SARAH

KAY P. DAWSON

THANK YOU

Thank you for purchasing *SARAH* - I hope you enjoy the story!

Sign up for my newsletter on my website at KAYPDAWSON.COM to get sales information, deals and details about all new releases - plus free books just for joining...INCLUDING THE DIARY WRITINGS OF CAROLINE - THE MOTHER TO THE WILDER SISTERS YOU ARE ABOUT TO MEET.

Don't forget to follow on your favourite social media sites too :)

This book is dedicated to my 2 wonderful girls, who have been patient and understanding while mom worked on writing and publishing this book.

And, of course to you....my readers. Without you, I wouldn't have anyone to share my stories with. Thank you for spending your time in the worlds I have created:)

CHAPTER 1

"Sarah! You need to think this through. Running off to marry a complete stranger just because one man has hurt you doesn't make any sense!"

"That isn't what I'm doing at all, and you know it, Beth!" Sarah stood perfectly still while she let the words sink in.

Beth's eyes grew bigger as she remembered their conversation months ago when Sarah had shared what she overheard between her mother and Alistair McConnell. Alistair was their father's friend and lawyer, and had spent a lot of time with all of them over the years while they were growing up.

Since their father's death, he'd stepped up to

help when he could, and they'd noticed him and their mother falling in love. When Sarah woke up in the middle of the night a few weeks ago, she overheard Alistair asking Caroline to marry him.

"So that's what this is about? You're going to answer an ad for a husband so that you don't have to feel responsible for Momma not marrying Mr. McConnell?" Beth sounded incredulous, even though she knew what Sarah was like, and truth be told, she wasn't surprised she'd made this decision.

When Alistair asked Caroline to marry him, Sarah had nearly leapt for joy. Her momma had experienced so much loss and pain in her life, enduring circumstances that would have surely killed someone weaker than her. Orphaned as a young girl, Caroline had been forced to work in a brothel to survive. That was how she'd met Sarah's father Thomas.

Their father had saved her from that life and set up an apartment for the family they had together, but he'd never given her his name or offered marriage. He was married to a society woman, and a union with Caroline would never have been accepted.

She'd raised the three girls mostly on her own,

and she deserved this chance for her own happy ending.

But Sarah had been surprised to hear her turn Alistair down, saying she couldn't marry in good conscience until she knew her daughters were all taken care of and settled into their own lives. She felt she owed them that much after the years they'd spent without a real father, and she worried marrying another man now might not be fair.

Caroline had told Alistair because of the pain their father had caused them, the girls might not ever want to marry or settle down. Not only that, but they were both already past marrying age, so she needed to continue just being their mother, guiding them to their own futures, without causing any more change or havoc in their lives.

Sarah had been left speechless. Momma would feel terrible knowing she'd overheard this.

She also knew her Momma was fierce, and if she ever felt that Sarah was marrying because of what she'd heard, she would never let it happen.

That's why she had to make sure her mother believed she was heading out West to meet a man she hoped she'd end up marrying for love.

"I've been writing to Hank for quite a few weeks now, ever since we got back to town after

Everly and Ben's wedding. I saw our sister find true love by answering an ad for a mail order bride, and there's no reason to believe the same won't happen for me." She lifted her chin a couple inches higher as she stared at her sister, daring her to argue. "And, when I tell Momma, she'll never know any different. As far as she will ever know, I've fallen in love with him already."

Sarah watched her younger sister roll her eyes. She tried to remain calm on the outside, even though inside she was just as unsure as Beth about what she was planning.

"Hank seems like a nice man who needs a wife. I'm sure in time I'll be able to love him." She tried to convince her sister as much as herself of the truth in her words.

Sarah almost laughed at the expression on Beth's face. Her jaw was hanging open as she struggled to find words that would explain how much she didn't believe a single word she had just heard.

Finally deciding there were no words that could be said, Beth just laughed out loud.

"Am I supposed to believe the Sarah I've always known to be a hopeless romantic, will be content to find a kind man who she'll possibly love in time? I don't think I've heard anything so ridiculous in my whole life."

Turning her back on her younger sister, Sarah looked out the window. Knowing Beth was right wasn't helping her right now. She needed to do this. Their older sister Everly had gone off to marry for the security of her family. Now it was her turn to do the same thing to ensure the happiness of her mother.

Beth came over and put her hand on Sarah's shoulder. "And, I don't think Momma will believe it either," she softly added.

"Momma would feel terrible to think you're doing this just for her. And anyway -- what about me? I'm still here, so it's not like she can run off and get married like you're hoping!"

Sarah turned back around to face Beth. "Well, that's why you're coming with me."

Again, Beth was left with no words as she stared back at her as though she'd just grown another head.

"Don't look at me like that, Beth. You're going to come with me, like I did for Everly when she went out to meet her future husband. Then, you can stay with me and we'll find you work to do out there so that Momma can be free to marry Mr.

McConnell. You know you loved it out West when you went to Everly's wedding. We can find you work keeping houses or teaching in a school -- maybe you can even find work in a stable like you do here. The people are much more accepting of women working, because the jobs need to get done and there aren't enough men to do them out there."

Beth sat down on the chair and put her arms on her legs while she tried to understand everything Sarah was saying.

Sarah knew this was her chance to convince her. "I need a chaperone, and you know you aren't happy here. You've always loved working with horses, and you'd be free of the past we have to live with here, where everyone knows how we grew up. It's different out West. Everyone gets to have a fresh start. And, you'll have me and Everly -- she and Ben just live a half day's ride from Mulder Creek."

Sarah watched the expression on Beth's face change to one of excitement. She knew her sister was too wild to stay here in Chicago where women were expected to act "proper" and "civilized". And, she had to convince her to come with her in order to give their mother the freedom to get married. Sarah desperately wanted to do this for her, because Momma deserved this chance to be happy.

Sarah crouched down in front of Beth. "Please, Beth. Everly risked everything to marry a stranger for us. It's my turn now to do this for Momma. And, I know you want the same thing. This will be our chance to do something good for her, to repay her for everything she's done for us. We'll look after each other, and I know Ben will keep an eye on us too, so we won't need to worry about being all alone. I've sent a letter to Everly to tell Ben to meet us when we get off the train, so he can make sure Hank is a good man for us to stay with."

She could tell by Beth's face she was convinced. She grabbed her sister's shoulders and pulled her in for a hug. "It will be wonderful, Beth! Now, we just have to convince Momma."

TIRED of tossing and turning while sleep eluded her, Sarah got up and went to the small room that served as kitchen, dining and sitting room in their small apartment. Making herself some tea, she walked over and sat in the chair by the window, listening to the rain fall on the roof outside.

They'd decided to wait until morning to tell their mother what they had planned. Sarah knew Momma wouldn't be happy about it, but as long as she believed it was for love, she was sure she wouldn't stop her.

She looked around the tiny apartment that had been home to her mother and sisters all these years, recalling memories of happy times mixed together with some of the more painful memories that had occurred between those walls. Her mother had done everything to make sure the three girls had happiness, and she knew how hard it'd been for her.

Her father had been in and out of their lives. Sometimes it would seem like he wanted to try being a father to them, while other times the pain he left when he walked out the door to go back to his "real" family, as they'd always called them, cut them straight through to the heart.

She'd always tried to stay positive, believing the good in her father, even when she could see the hatred building in her sisters towards the man who would never give them his name.

But, she'd never told her sisters just how much

her own heart had been hurting. She never wanted to let on because she felt that if she did, the anger and pain her sisters were feeling would consume them. She believed she was the only one who could keep them from losing all hope, and she needed to try and keep them all happy.

She was the "happy" sister, the one who believed in fairy tales.

So many times, she'd seen her mother cry when their father left, but often she thought she could see pain in his eyes too when he had to say good-bye. She always wanted to believe the best in people, even when the truth seemed otherwise.

Watching what her parents went through, never living together as husband and wife as they wanted, made her terrified of that same fate. She read the romance books, even while her sisters poked fun at her, saying romances like the ones in books didn't actually exist. They were already both so bitter over what they'd witnessed with their parents, neither one of them believed in true love.

That was, until her older sister Everly had answered an ad just a few short months ago for a mail order bride. Now, Everly had found her true love, and while Beth was convinced it was just a one-time stroke of luck, Sarah believed it could happen for her, too.

She even thought at one time she might have found her true love, only to realize all those years of reading the fairy tales and romance books had caused her to see things that weren't really there.

She curled her legs up under her while she wrapped a throw around her shoulders to stop the chill from the room. She hated when thoughts of Jake interrupted her sleep, and she got so angry at herself for letting him still consume so much of her thoughts.

Jake was the cousin to Ben, her sister's new husband. Sarah had gone out to stay with Everly to support her sister, and to make sure she was safe. Everly never wanted to get married, and Sarah knew if she'd sent Everly on her own, she likely would have turned and ran straight back home without ever giving it a chance.

What Sarah hadn't counted on were the feelings she started to have for a man who'd make it clear he never wanted to fall in love or get married.

When she'd first met Jake on the front porch of Ben and Everly's house, she felt her breath taken away, just like in the books she'd read. She thought from his expression he felt much the same way.

Over the weeks, they'd spent time together, but it seemed instead of getting closer to him, he was pushing her further away.

Each time they were together, he was angry with her over something she didn't even know she'd done. No matter how hard she tried to figure out what she could do to make things work between them, he wouldn't let her in.

She'd held onto the hope that when it was time for her to leave, he would realize he had feelings for her and ask her to stay. Her heart broke when it never happened. When she said her good-byes to her sister, brother-in-law and the other family gathered around the morning she was set to leave, Jake had merely tipped his hat down with a simple, "Have a safe trip home." He looked deep into her eyes before he turned and jumped onto his horse.

Her last memories of him were nothing but a cloud of dust as he rode out of the yard.

She came home needing to mend her broken heart and take her future into her own hands. She wouldn't end up with a man like Jake who'd never offer her more than what her father had given her own mother. She thought she'd have time to find someone who could give her the love she was craving, but hearing her mother and Alistair talking that night had changed everything.

She had to do something now, and the ad Hank put in the paper seemed to be the answer she'd been looking for.

Hank's ad said he'd lost his wife and needed a woman to fill his heart. He sounded so heart-broken and alone, Sarah felt compelled to write to him. They'd sent a few letters back and forth, and he seemed genuine and thoughtful. She couldn't believe he was real -- he sounded almost too good to be true.

He lived in Mulder Creek, which was just a half day's ride from High Ridge, Wyoming, where Everly lived. He had his own ranch, no children and was looking for a young wife who could make his house more home-like and possibly give him children to love.

Sarah felt a sadness in him, and wanted to be the one to help him heal. And, if the truth be known, she wanted to try healing herself as well.

She'd already set the plan into motion, agreeing to come out to Mulder Creek to meet him. She signed an agreement he sent saying she'd stay for at least two weeks to see if they were suited. He said he had a sister who lived with him who would ensure everything was "proper" and she wouldn't need to be uncomfortable staying with a strange man.

The way he was concerned for her need for propriety gave Sarah hope Hank would be a good man. But, just to make sure, she sent the letter asking Ben to meet them. Everly was expecting a baby any day now, but she hoped it would work out that Ben could take a day to ensure their safety when they got off the train.

In only two more days, she would leave to meet her future husband. It made her sad to leave home, but she still hoped she'd find love the way Everly had with Ben.

And she hoped Hank could heal her heart and give her the future she'd always dreamed about.

CHAPTER 2

"I've had a lot of interest in the new stallion I picked up on my last trip back east. He adds a powerful lineage to our herd, and will be able to bring in some good money for breeding fees." Jake was sitting on his cousin Ben's front porch enjoying a visit as he often did. Before Ben was married, he'd come over just about every evening, but now he only came over a few times a week to discuss business and to visit with Ben's nieces who lived with him.

Everly came out the door after putting the girls to bed. Jake watched as Ben reached his hand out for her, then pulled her over to sit down on his lap. She put her arm around his shoulders, and smiled down at him.

"How are you feeling?" Ben asked her. "Make sure you aren't overdoing it. Maybe you should go in to bed."

Jake smiled as Everly responded, "I'm not the first woman to have a baby. I'm fine. If I wasn't feeling well, I'd go and rest."

Everly looked towards Jake. "Can I get you something to drink Jake?"

"No, I'm fine. I wouldn't want Ben getting worried about you not having the strength to carry a glass out onto the porch!" Jake joked. Ben had been fussing over Everly for months since finding out she was having a baby, and he knew how much it annoyed Everly. They joked about it often, which Ben didn't seem to find as amusing as they did.

"Well then, I think I'll head into bed. I admit I do feel a bit tired tonight, so I will say good night."

She leaned down and kissed Ben. He helped her up, then held the door for her as she went. As he watched, Jake felt a bit of jealousy ripple through him. He shook it off, knowing that he'd never have a love like what Ben and Everly had. He wasn't looking for anything like that anyway.

As Everly went in the door, Jake saw her nod towards him with a questioning look. He couldn't help but notice Ben's answering shake of his head as he closed the door behind her.

"Do you want to tell me what that was all about?" he asked Ben as he sat back down beside him.

Ben shifted in his seat and tried to change the subject. "Have you thought of a name for your new stallion?"

Jake knew when Ben was stalling about something, and he could tell this was one of those times. The air around them had suddenly got thick after Everly had gone inside, and Jake was determined to find out what was going on.

"Well, I'm naming him Atlas, but I'm sure that isn't really what you're supposed to talk to me about, so you may as well just spit it out."

Ben pushed his hands through his hair and finally lifted his eyes to meet Jake's. "Sarah's on her way out to Mulder Creek to get married," he finally blurted out.

Jake kept his face completely still as Ben watched him closely to gauge his reaction.

"But, the problem is, the man she's heading out here to meet is not who he's made himself out to be. She sent Everly a letter that only arrived yesterday saying she's been writing to a man in Mulder Creek who was looking for a wife. Apparently they have been writing for awhile, and he's made a lot of false promises and lies to her over those months."

Jake still hadn't moved a muscle as he let the words sink in. All he kept hearing in his head were the words about Sarah getting married.

"Well, she'll have to find out the hard way that love isn't something that just falls in your lap. And, putting your trust in someone is never a good idea." He said the words that didn't even sound right in his own ears, but he didn't know how else to react.

"You can't be serious, Jake!" Ben sounded incredulous that he'd be so flippant about a woman he knew Jake had cared about, even if he wouldn't admit it to himself.

"Don't you want to know who the man is? As soon as Everly told me the name, the skin on my arms began to crawl."

"I'm not interested. What Sarah chooses to do with her life is of no concern to me." He started to stand up to leave, but not before Ben let him know who the man was anyway.

"Hank Barlow."

The name echoed across the quiet of the evening as Jake let the words sink in.

Hank Barlow was well known in the area, having a father who'd been under suspicion for assaulting and possibly even killing his own wife, not to mention the fact that Hank himself had been responsible for Jake's fiancé leaving him the day of their wedding.

Hank and his father, Stewart Barlow, were his biggest competition in the horse-breeding business, and were unscrupulous snakes who would do anything to get what they wanted. It was like they'd made it their life's purpose to destroy Jake's.

He sat back down in stunned quiet. "How the hell did she get mixed up with the likes of those two?" he asked himself out loud.

"I think they somehow found out her connection to you. Who knows how, but I have no doubt they found out, and they made sure Sarah saw an ad from them she couldn't resist answering." Ben replied, even though he'd known Jake wasn't really asking for an answer.

"Well, they're wrong. There was never anything between us. Nothing more than a girl's fancy that she was falling in love with a man who'd never be suited to her."

He got back up and started pacing the porch. "I've always made it clear to everyone that I have no intentions of ever marrying. And, no matter what Sarah might have been thinking was between us, it would never have been what she deserved. I'm not the marrying kind."

Ben stood up and looked Jake straight in the eye. "Jake, you have to let go of the anger you have about marriage. It didn't work out for you the first time you tried it, but that doesn't mean it isn't for you. You were lucky to be rid of Anna, anyway. A woman that'd be swayed so easily to another man isn't the kind of woman you'd want to be tied to for the rest of your life."

Jake could feel the heat rising in his face as he tried not to remember the humiliation and anger he'd felt the day he was supposed to marry Anna, the woman he thought he loved---- and who he thought loved him. But, she'd always only been after money, and he was glad he'd found that out before any vows had been said.

Hank had convinced her to run off with him. At the time, Barlow Ranch had grown to be one of the largest in the area, and Hank had flashed his money to convince her to leave Jake for him. Jake was still just getting started at growing his herd and didn't have the funds to compete with Hank.

It didn't matter that Hank had no interest in her anyway, and was only using her to get at Jake as revenge for becoming a threat to their business. After the broken engagement, he told Anna he'd never had any feelings for her. The damage had been done though, and when she came crawling back to Jake begging for forgiveness and desperate for him to still marry her, he'd told her it was over.

From that day on, Jake had vowed he'd never let himself be put into a position where he could be hurt by a woman. And he certainly would never say any vows that would tie him to a woman for life.

He shrugged his shoulders while he leaned against a post on the edge of the porch. He glanced over at his cousin who was pushing his hands through his hair in frustration. "Whatever the reasons, and whatever she's doing now, it isn't my concern." He said words that he hoped would convince himself were true.

"Jake! I'm supposed meet Sarah and Beth at the train when it gets to Mulder Creek on Wednesday. That's only two days away, and I don't want to leave Everly alone now, not when she's this close to having the baby. Sarah wanted someone there to make sure the man she's meeting is suitable, and you and I both know he is nowhere near close to being suitable, or even safe, for her!"

"Jake, you have to go in my place." Ben grabbed his arm to stop him, as he shook his head and pushed himself away from the post. "Just listen -- I wouldn't even think of asking you if it weren't for the baby. I was going to get Andrew to go in my place, but he left this morning to check out a horse he heard about down in Colorado and won't be back for quite a few days."

Andrew was Sarah's stepbrother, and although they hadn't all grown up together, they'd finally had the chance to get to know one another over the past few months. He was working with Jake and Ben on their ranch, and was a partner in business dealings with their horse herd. He'd been called down to see about buying a horse they'd been looking at, and had to leave before Ben got the chance to ask if he could meet the women when they arrived.

Ben continued, "And, you can say what you want. I don't believe that you'd ever leave Sarah to get hurt. You aren't that kind of man."

Jake growled low in his throat as he looked at

21

his cousin's smug look. He knew Jake would never let anyone get hurt if he could do something to help, and he also knew that no matter what he said, he did care about Sarah enough to not want to see her get hurt.

As the men stood looking at each other, with just the sounds of the night closing in around them, they suddenly heard a glass shattering in the house. Ben turned and ran inside, with Jake close behind.

Jake saw Everly standing near the table, with a broken water glass on the floor. She was bent over clutching her stomach, and she looked up at them with a terrified expression on her face. Ben raced over to her and swept her up in his arms, carrying her up to their room.

As he listened to Ben offer reassuring words to his wife, Jake yelled out that he'd run into town to get the doctor. He jumped off the porch and onto his horse, racing out of the yard towards town. He loved Ben like a brother, and he was feeling a mix of worry for Everly that everything would be all right, along with excitement knowing he'd soon be an uncle again.

And, as he flew towards town, he couldn't help thinking how he was now going to have to be the one meeting Sarah when she arrived. He wasn't happy about it, but Ben was right. He couldn't let her end up with a man like Hank Barlow.

He just hoped when she saw him there, she didn't decide to run off with Hank anyway just to get even. He didn't even know if he'd blame her if she did.

CHAPTER 3

The train's whistle pierced through Sarah's thoughts, as she remembered the trip she'd made with Everly just a few months ago. At that time, she was excited to be off on an adventure, never once realizing how scared her sister had to have been feeling. She looked over at Beth who was eagerly looking out the window watching the scenery racing by, and wished that she could feel that same excitement again.

In truth, she was feeling so apprehensive about it all now, but she didn't have the heart to admit it. After all, it was her idea that set all of this into motion. She'd dragged her sister into this, and now she was responsible.

When she told her mother, she never admitted

to hearing her and Mr. McConnell talking. But, she'd let it slip out that now they could get married without having to worry about the girls, and that was enough for her mother to start questioning why she'd ever think that. She tried to cover and make up a story saying she was just guessing, but she knew her Momma knew something was up.

Her mother hadn't seemed happy about her decision to come out West, and it'd taken a lot of convincing to allow it. She'd had to promise Ben would be there to look after them when they got off the train to stop her and Alistair from coming with them. She knew if they did, it would just cause more worry, so she'd been adamant they didn't need to come.

"I just can't believe how green and beautiful everything out here looks away from the city!" Beth was in awe of the view out her window. She'd been out once before for her older sister's wedding, but she still couldn't seem to get over how amazing everything looked after growing up in the city.

Not hearing any response, Beth looked over at Sarah. "Are you all right? I've never known you to be so quiet in your life."

Sarah smiled at her. "I'm fine. Just a little nervous I guess."

Beth pretended to act shocked. "You mean Sarah, the girl who believes everyone is wonderful and life is an adventure to be grasped with open arms, is actually feeling a little nervous?"

Sarah hit her sister lightly on the arm, laughing at her weak attempt to make her feel better. "Very funny. Yes, even people like me feel nervous sometimes."

She looked down at her hands folded in her lap while the train slowed to stop in a small town to pick up more passengers. Sensing how truly worried she was feeling, Beth reached over and took one of her hands in hers.

"Everything will be fine, Sarah. I'm here with you, and Everly and Ben will be too. No one is going to let you end up doing anything you'll regret, or let you get hurt. That's a promise."

Hearing the words, Sarah had to fight to stop the tears from escaping her eyes. She didn't even understand why she was feeling so upset. This was exactly what she'd always dreamed of — heading out to meet a man she'd fall in love with, and have her happy ever after.

She watched as a young woman close to her age

stepped onto the train. She couldn't help but wonder if she was heading out to a new life of her own, and how she was feeling. She was a nice looking girl, but her eyes seemed so scared, as she looked around the train for somewhere to sit. It didn't seem fair that women had to sometimes take such risks to make their lives follow the dreams they had.

Turning her head to look out the window as the train started to pull away again, she couldn't help but notice the dust being kicked up by wagons going past on the road, filled with couples who seemed so happy together. Her eyes followed a couple in front of the town's only store, who were laughing as the man lifted the woman out of the wagon and set her on the ground.

She thought back to a time when she was in Wyoming with her sister, and a man had lifted her out of their wagon and set her on the ground. She'd looked deep into his eyes as he lifted her, feeling like her heart had tumbled straight out of her chest.

Her arms folded across her chest, and she sighed as she turned her head away from the window, shaking her head of the memories that were haunting her thoughts. Today she should be feeling excitement for the new life she was heading toward, not bringing up memories of the past.

Her sister noticed where her eyes had been watching, and knowing her as well as she did, she knew her thoughts weren't on the man she was heading out to meet.

"You still have feelings for him, don't you, Sarah?" Beth quietly asked her, the whistle of the train as it picked up speed almost drowning out her words.

"I'm fine, Beth. It will take some time, but Jake always made it clear to me he wouldn't ever marry, for any reason, so I need to move on. He obviously didn't have the feelings for me I thought he did, and I was foolish enough to make myself believe there was more than there really was between us."

"Anyway, we are now only a few hours away from Mulder Creek. The next stop is ours, so let's start thinking of the exciting adventures that are sure to be coming our way!" Sarah tried to convince herself as much as Beth the excitement was real. She just wished she could truly believe it.

As the next few hours seemed to fly by as fast the scenery outside, the niggling worry that Sarah had been feeling, as though something wasn't quite right, started to grow. Not wanting to let her sister know just how worried she was, and not willing to admit that maybe this wasn't a good idea, she tried to push the thoughts out of her head.

She could feel the train slowing, and her sister was excitedly telling her about everything she was seeing out the window in this new town that would be her home. She was talking about seeing a store, a small little church just up the road, a mill, a hotel, so much smaller than Chicago, but so much more lovely in her eyes. Sarah smiled, glad that Beth was able to feel so much excitement about what they were doing.

She heard Beth gasp as they pulled up to the station, and wondering what she was looking at now, Sarah peeked over Beth's lap to see what she could possibly be staring at out the window with her mouth hanging open. Nothing could have prepared her to see Jake standing on the station platform, looking angrier than she ever remembered seeing him before.

"What is he doing here?" Beth almost shrieked the words.

"I have no idea, but I will not let him ruin this for me." Standing up with a sense of calmness she wasn't sure she was really feeling, she grabbed her bag and started walking toward the door. Beth had to hurry to catch up as she started going down the steps.

If Jake was here to cause trouble, she was going to make sure she was ready.

Stepping off the train, her eyes immediately found Jake. She thought she noticed his face soften for a moment, but she knew she was only imagining something she wanted to see. Unable to move her eyes from his, she was grateful to have her sister, who took her elbow and started moving her toward where Jake was standing beside two other men.

"Hello, Jake. I'm surprised to see you here. I'd thought Ben was coming to meet us at the train." She could almost feel her knees starting to give out beneath her as she felt emotions she'd thought she was finally over after all this time. Why did he still have the same effect on her? Why couldn't she just hate him like she wanted to do?

"Hello, Sarah, it's nice to see you." Jake took his hat off as he bowed just a bit too dramatically for her to believe he was sincere. "Unfortunately, Ben was busy as Everly had her baby just last night, so he didn't feel he could leave her. He asked me to come in his place."

"Everly had her baby?" Beth shouted, almost

pushing Sarah off the platform as she let go of her arm and rushed past her to get closer to hear Jake. "What did she have? Is she all right?"

Jake smiled as he thought of the new baby. "They had a boy, and everyone was doing well when I left. They named him Thomas."

Sarah was surprised that Everly had named the baby after their father, but she also knew Everly had told her that if not for the terms he'd set in his will, she would never have found the happiness she had with Ben.

The man standing directly beside Jake finally stepped forward, putting his hand out towards her. "Sorry to interrupt the reunion, but I'm Hank Barlow, the man you have been writing to."

Sarah noticed the hostile look that passed between Hank and Jake as she finally took notice of the other men. As she shook Hank's hand, she couldn't help but think how handsome he was. For the first time since she got on the train, she actually thought maybe this would be something which could work out very well for her.

"Oh Hank, I'm so sorry! I didn't realize you were here as well. Please forgive my rudeness!"

"Not to worry. I'm used to rudeness when Jake Montgomery is around." He smiled to try to soothe

the undercurrent of anger that'd come through in his words. "And this is my father, Stewart," he introduced as he pulled the other man forward to meet her.

Sarah noticed the look of fury on Jake's face as he was watching the exchange before him. She was so confused about why he was mad, and she was sure it wasn't just because she was meeting another man. So, she couldn't understand why he looked like he wanted to kill Hank Barlow right there on the train's platform.

"I understand your need to have someone here to meet you at the train to ensure your safety; however, I assure you that both you and your sister will be in good hands with us." There was something about Hank's father that set Sarah's skin crawling as she shook his hand, but she was sure it was just her nerves playing havoc with her mind.

When she saw that Jake was clenching his fists tightly looking like he was about to strangle the man, she wondered if there was more to it.

"Jake, you can go home and tell Sarah's sister that she's fine and will be taken care of with the highest regard." Hank practically sneered at Jake as he said the words.

"There's no way in hell I'm leaving these

women in your care Hank, and you know it." Sarah could see that Jake was almost shaking he was so angry, as he slowly moved closer to Hank.

Scared of what was about to unfold in front of her, she looked at her sister for a clue about what she should do. Beth was standing, staring in confusion, and Sarah knew she was going to have to stop this before things got worse.

"Does someone want to tell me exactly what's going on here between you two?" She almost screamed the words to try and make them hear her, as they were both staring each other down unaware of anyone else around them anymore.

"Nothing you need to worry about my dear. Jake will be leaving, and you'll be staying with me. After all, I've paid good money for tickets to get you out here, and there's no way you will be going off with the likes of him." Hank's voice scared her as he spoke so calmly, while she could tell he was just as angry as Jake.

"Doesn't matter what you paid, Barlow. She's coming back to High Ridge with me, and there's nothing you can do to stop it."

"Hmmmmm...Sounds like this little woman might mean an awful lot to you. I can't imagine how terrible you'll feel to see her marrying me." It seemed as though Hank was taunting Jake, and Sarah was starting to get angry. How could they be talking like this about her as if she was some prize they both wanted to win, and as if she wasn't even standing there beside them!

Sensing that things were heading into a dangerous direction, Beth noticed a man walking a half a block away that seemed to be wearing a badge. Hoping it was a sheriff, Sarah watched her run toward the man.

"Doesn't matter what I do or don't feel about her, she isn't marrying you." Noticing Jake moving closer to Hank, Sarah started to panic.

"Stop it!" she shouted, as she pushed herself in front of Jake. "What are you doing, Jake? I came out here to meet Hank; this has nothing to do with you!" She could feel tears running down her cheeks as the stress of the past few days finally got the better of her.

"And you!" She turned toward Hank, pointing her finger at him. "How dare you say that I owe you for sending me money for a ticket! I came out here under the impression that we were going to meet and see if we were suited before making any decisions."

She walked over, picked up her bag that had

been dropped onto the platform, and turned back toward the men who were finally paying attention to her.

"I'll be staying in a hotel, and I won't be leaving with either one of you! You're both acting like spoiled children, and I won't be a part of it."

She turned to storm away before she had a chance to change her mind. Hank's words stopped her in her tracks, "Oh, I'm afraid you will be coming with me, my dear. You signed a contract saying you would, and I don't reckon I'd be too happy to see you breaking it."

Stewart Barlow stepped toward her. "You don't want to cross a Barlow, young lady. We always make sure we get what we're owed."

Sarah looked at Jake with fear in her eyes, hoping she was somehow hearing things wrong. But the look on his face left her with no doubt in her mind that the man she'd been writing to, and who she'd come out here hoping to marry, was not the man he'd led her to believe.

CHAPTER 4

"Is there a problem here?" A man's voice that she didn't recognize ripped through her thoughts. She turned to look at who'd walked up behind her, and her legs almost buckled with relief as she saw Beth with a man who appeared to be a sheriff. He wore a badge, and had a large cowboy hat on his head. She couldn't help notice the scar that ran from his jaw line down his neck, and she briefly wondered what had happened to cause it.

"Nothing that concerns you, Dixon. I'm here to pick up my future wife, and Jake here was just leaving." Hank wasn't backing down, but Sarah also felt some relief as she looked over at Jake and somehow knew he wasn't about to just leave her here alone.

"Well, this young lady here seems to believe my help is needed, so until I hear the whole story, no one is going anywhere." The man looked to Sarah. "Can you please explain what's going on? Your sister came to me worried that something bad was about to happen between these two men." He spoke so kindly, she almost choked on the tears that were threatening to start flowing again.

"I don't know. I've been writing to Hank and had agreed to come out and meet him. My brother-in-law, Ben Montgomery, was supposed to meet me at the train to make sure Hank was safe for me to stay with while we decided if we would be suited for marriage. He couldn't make it, so his cousin Jake came in his place. But for some reason everyone is arguing, and now Hank and his father are saying I have to go with them no matter what...." She knew she wasn't making sense, and the words were tumbling out of her mouth faster than her thoughts could keep up.

As she tried to explain everything that seemed to be going so wrong, despite all the hopes she had coming out here, the tears that had been threatening to spill over finally started to escape. She

KAY P. DAWSON

turned her head away as she tried to get herself back under control.

Beth came over and put an arm around her shoulder, as she glared over toward Hank and his father. "These men are trying to say Sarah has to leave with them -- that she signed some kind of contract saying she would. However, after seeing how they've all behaved since we arrived, she has decided she'd like to have some time to make a more informed decision without having to stay with any of them." Beth spoke for her, allowing her a few minutes to regain her composure.

Sarah looked back toward Jake, and she thought she noticed his eyes watching her with concern. But she knew all she was really seeing was anger with her for being inconvenienced. Her cheeks started to heat up as she realized the mess she'd created for all of them.

"Unfortunately, Miss Wilder did sign a contract stating that if she agreed to take the money we sent for her ticket to come out here, she was agreeing to the marriage. If she assumed otherwise, or if she read more into the words I put into the letters, then I do apologize. However, the fact remains that unless there's some reason that she can't be married to me, when she arrives in Mulder Creek, she is bound to marry me." Hank sneered towards Jake, as he reached into the pocket of his coat, pulling out a piece of paper.

The sheriff reached out as Hank handed him the piece of paper. Sarah watched him read it, as her heart sank. She recognized the paper, and she saw her signature on the bottom. The paper she'd signed without reading all the way through, the one Hank had said was merely an agreement saying she'd stay for at least two weeks before deciding if they were suited for marriage, was now being used to force her into marriage.

"Is this your signature, ma'am?" The sheriff looked pained as he slowly lifted his head and asked her.

"Well, it is, but that's not what he said I was signing!" Sarah felt panicked now as she looked around at the faces staring at her. Once again, her immaturity and habit of rushing into things without thinking was coming back to haunt her. Why didn't she think things through? Why couldn't she be more like her sisters, more mature and not so quick to believe that everyone was good and truthful?

She looked toward Jake. For some reason, she felt like he could fix this. He looked at her with a blank look, making her realize even he couldn't fix this. She walked to a bench that was on the platform behind her. She just needed a minute to try and gather her thoughts.

She sat down, putting her hands out as she spoke. "He told me it was just an agreement to stay with him for a minimum of two weeks to see if we were suited! He said he has a sister who'll be staying with us! I just assumed I was agreeing to stay for at least that long in exchange for the ticket money for me and my sister!" She was feeling lightheaded as she looked at the expressions on the faces around her.

"Sarah, didn't you read the paper before you signed it?" Beth quietly came over, crouching down in front of her. She couldn't even speak as she shook her head, shame at the knowledge that everything everyone always said about her being too trusting, too much of a believer in fairy tales, was now being proven to be true.

She turned pleading eyes to Jake. He walked over to her and stood beside her while he turned to face Hank. "Seems to me you gave her some false promises and I'd think in the eyes of the law that would make any contract void." He looked over toward the sheriff for support.

Before the sheriff could speak, Hank's father, Stewart, spoke up. "Doesn't matter what she was told. She signed a paper that had it all written out for her if she'd just taken the time to read it. Not our fault she is a simpering fool of a girl who would agree to run off half-way around the country with some silly romantic notions in her head!"

Jake plunged at Stewart, and if not for the sheriff stepping between them, Sarah was sure he would've knocked him straight on the ground.

"It's your fool son who put those romantic notions in her head in the first place!" Sarah noticed he was shaking with anger, and she was glad he was on her side. She wouldn't want to be the one crossing Jake Montgomery.

Sarah looked at Hank and wondered how she'd ever thought he was handsome, even for a brief moment. He was practically sneering at her as he walked closer to her, reaching his hand out. "So, I guess you and I should start getting better acquainted, my darling." Sarah heard a sound that resembled a growl before she even had a chance to realize what was happening.

Jake had roared past the sheriff, and now had Hank on the ground. His hands were around the man's throat, and Sarah raced over to stop him from doing something that would get him in more trouble.

"Jake, stop! Let him go!" She was pulling on his arms, trying to get him off the man he was holding on the ground.

By now, the sheriff was there, and he somehow managed to pull Jake back up and off Hank. Stewart raced over and pulled his son up off the ground. "You'll be sorry you ever messed with us, Jake Montgomery." Stewart's eyes bulged out of his head as he spoke, while Hank had a smug look on his face as he brushed his jacket sleeves off.

"You'll not lay one filthy finger on this woman." Jake's shoulders were heaving as he spoke the words between clenched teeth.

"Well, my signed contract says otherwise. And now, I might just have to see you arrested for causing me bodily harm." Hank was standing at a safe distance, with the sheriff between them.

The sheriff put his hand on Jake's arm, holding him back from more confrontation. "Your contract states that she would marry you unless she was unable to for any reason, if I remember correctly. Is that right?" The sheriff was still holding Jake back, while Sarah wondered what he was getting at.

"Yes, that's correct. But there's no reason whatsoever that Miss Wilder can't marry me, so she'll be coming with me." Hank's eyes scared Sarah, as she noticed a look of wild fury, and she knew she'd never be safe if she had to leave with him.

"If she was already married, that would make her unable to marry you, Hank." The sheriff glanced toward Jake, and Sarah noticed his jaw clench. She saw him look over at her, and the anger in his eyes was directed straight at her. She didn't understand what was happening, but if the sheriff had a way for her to get out of this contract, she was ready to do whatever she had to.

"Yes, but she isn't married..." Hank realized at that moment what the sheriff was hinting at. He flung his head back as he laughed, "Jake won't marry her. He's sworn off ever getting married, and I'm sure he won't be getting married to some girl who's backed him into a corner!"

"Besides, no woman would ever want to be saddled to a man like him. I happen to know quite well that he's already found that out once." Again, the sheriff had to hold Jake as Hank kept talking.

Jake looked at Sarah, then back to the sheriff.

"Do you have the authority to do this?" he asked him with his teeth still clenched. The sheriff nodded his head, as both Hank and Stewart stood there laughing.

"Well, Sarah. Looks like you're getting your wish. You came out west for a husband, and you're about to get one." Jake grabbed her arm and pulled her over toward him. Before she even knew what was happening, the sheriff was already speaking and joining them in marriage.

As the last words were being spoken, Jake pulled her close to him and leaned his head down to hers. She'd never seen such anger in anyone's eyes, and she was almost sure he was more dangerous at that moment than even Hank Barlow could be. "And since I now have myself a wife, I hope you will allow me this chance to seal it with a kiss..."

CHAPTER 5

*H*is lips crushed hers, and Jake knew he was hurting her. But the anger he was feeling overshadowed everything else. Thanks to her foolish romantic notions, he was now tied to this woman for the rest of his life. He'd done what he could to keep her safe from that snake Hank, and even as he kissed her, full of anger, he knew that for whatever reason, he would never have let her go off with any other man anyway.

Something wet pooled on his lip, and he suddenly realized the woman he was forcing his lips on was crying. Pulling back, he felt something soften inside his heart as he looked into her eyes. Gently lifting his hands to her cheek, he brushed the tears away that were escaping. She looked terrified, and he realized that even though she hadn't thought everything through, she hadn't asked for any of this either.

He also realized that he was going to have to be very careful around this woman. She'd somehow wound her way into his heart, and he was going to have to do everything he could to keep his distance. He wouldn't be hurt by a woman again.

He pulled his hat down as he turned back to the people who were all still gathered on the street in front of the train station.

"Like I said, Barlow. You won't be laying one finger on her." With that, he took her by the hand and started dragging her over to where he'd tied Atlas. When he'd come out to meet the train, he decided to bring the new stallion because he knew he would make the trip with ease.

Sarah was pulling back, telling him to wait so she could grab her bags, but he was determined to get her out of there before Barlow could do any more harm. Beth was running behind, grabbing their bags while the sheriff tried to help.

"Fine looking horse you have there, Mont-gomery." Jake could feel the skin crawl on his neck as he realized too late the mistake he'd made bringing Atlas anywhere near the Barlow men. He slowly turned to face Hank, as he walked over toward where he stood next to his horse. Stewart wasn't far behind, and together they walked around the horse, eyeing him up as they stroked his black coat.

Sensing tension, Atlas started to paw at the ground, while he snorted loudly at the men looking at him.

"Looks like he'd make a great addition to any herd for breeding stock." Jake still hadn't said anything, but as the other men spoke, he was clenching his fists waiting to see what they were going to say next.

This time it was Stewart who spoke. "Would be a darn shame for a newly married man to have to spend time locked up for assault, especially on his wedding night..." Stewart chuckled as he continued stroking Atlas, never taking his eyes off Jake.

"What do you want, Barlow?" Jake spoke through clenched teeth, growling low as he moved closer to the man who was speaking.

Not missing his cue, Hank added, "My throat still bears the marks where Montgomery had his hands." For extra emphasis, he put his hands up to rub at his collar.

Suddenly, Jake started to feel like hands were

clenching around his own throat as he started to suspect what Hank Barlow and his father were hinting at.

"I reckon we could be persuaded not to press any charges for the right price, wouldn't you agree, son?" Stewart looked at Hank with a gleam in his eye, while Hank was nodding his head.

"I would rather go to jail than let you leave with this horse, so you can both head over to your own damn horses you rode in on. Those are the only animals you will be leaving with today." Jake was not about to let the two of them get their hands on his prize stallion that he'd just bought. He didn't care if he did have to go to jail for assaulting that snake.

"Well, perhaps you'd rather spend some time locked up, but I'm sure your lovely new bride wouldn't enjoy the comforts our local courthouse offers. We have to remember, there's also the matter of a contract being broken, and money we are owed for tickets and other amenities while these two ladies came out west."

Sarah jumped in. "I never knew what I was signing, and you know it! If you want to be paid for your tickets, I will send notice to my family lawyer and we'll have the money sent to you. Jake doesn't have to pay for my debts." She was seething with anger, but Jake knew that these men were not just going to let them go that easily. It wasn't about the money, and he knew it.

It was one thing for him to go to jail, but he wasn't about to let Sarah spend any time locked up because of a grudge these men had with him.

He reached up and undid the saddle on Atlas' back. He looked into the horse's eyes as he stroked its nose. "Don't worry boy, I'll get you back. This isn't over." He was sure the horse understood, and as he walked away with the saddle over his shoulder, the horse whinnied.

"No Jake! You can't let him have your horse." Sarah looked devastated, and she was running to Atlas and grabbing the reins. Hank pushed past her, almost knocking her over as he jumped up onto the horse's bare back. He was laughing as he started to turn the horse. "Told you, Montgomery. A Barlow always gets what he wants!"

As he pulled to turn the horse, Atlas sensed that something was wrong, and went up onto his hind legs, throwing Hank to the ground.

Jake never turned back as he walked away from the horse he had prized so much. He could hear Sarah still trying to convince him not to let them take the horse, but he knew the fight wasn't worth it right now. He just wanted to get Sarah and her sister back to High Ridge where he could dump them off for Ben to deal with. Then he'd be able to think and hopefully come up with a plan to get his horse back.

He also needed time to come to terms with the fact that, whether he liked it or not, he was now a married man.

SARAH RODE QUIETLY BESIDE BETH, while Jake rode further ahead on the trail. She knew how angry he was, and she didn't blame him one bit. She struggled to hold her tears back as she thought of all the trouble she'd caused for everyone since she got here.

Now Jake was stuck married to her, and she wasn't even sure she knew what had all happened back there in Mulder Creek. Everything happened so fast, and now it all just seemed like a jumbled mess in her mind. And, she had no idea how she was going to fix it.

Then, for Jake to end up losing his prize stallion was almost too tragic for her to think about.

She could work hard to show him she'd be a good wife for him, but she didn't think there was much she could do to replace his horse. Worse than that, now the Barlows -- Jake's biggest competition in the industry -- had the prized stallion for their own herd.

Nothing she could do would change that.

"Jake! Can we please slow down just a bit? We're tired, we're holding our bags on these horses, and quite frankly, I need to stop and attend to some business!" Beth was getting cranky, and Sarah could understand. She felt pretty much the same way, but she didn't dare ask Jake to stop.

They'd rented some mares from the stables in town to get home to High Ridge. Jake had said he'd have one of the hired hands bring them back the following day. Sarah could ride well enough, but not as good as both Jake and Beth, so she was getting a bit sore from having to ride so fast.

Jake turned and glanced back over his shoulder. Sarah couldn't help her heart from skipping a beat when her eyes met his, even after everything that'd happened since she arrived. His eyes seemed to look right into her soul, and heat spread through her body.

He shrugged his shoulders, reined his horse in

and hopped down from his saddle. Realizing he had no intention of helping her down, she tried to mirror her sister's movements as Beth easily brought her leg over and jumped down from the back of her horse. However, the fatigue from the day, along with the fact that she wasn't really a rider like her sister, worked against her.

As she fell, she could suddenly sense Jake right beside her. His arms reached out and caught her just as she was about to hit the ground.

"You really can't get enough of me having to save you, can you?" He looked annoyed, even while she thought she noticed a touch of fear in his eyes too.

Angrily, she pushed him away from her and brushed herself off. She knew how much he'd sacrificed for her today, and she was grateful. She was sorry for everything she had caused.

But, she was also getting tired of being reminded about it. She didn't set out to do any of this on purpose, and if she was ever going to get the chance to try making things right, he needed to let her apologize and move past it.

"Look, Jake. I know you're angry. And I certainly don't blame you one bit. I've caused you a tremendous amount of inconvenience today..."

"Inconvenience? Is that all you think has happened here today?" Jake fairly shouted the words as he inched his face closer to hers. "Inconvenience? Let me tell you something. I've not only had to give up my freedom, to be shackled to a woman who quite obviously doesn't ever think things through completely, for the rest of my life, but I've lost the one horse that most likely would've put our ranch on the map, to the biggest competition I have."

He pushed his face even closer, and Sarah could feel the heat from his breath as he continued. "I never wanted to be married, and just a few short hours ago, I wasn't. I was free to decide if I wanted to find someone to love and spend my life with. Now, that has been taken from me as quickly as the stallion I had such high hopes for." He stepped back from her and lowered his voice.

"So don't talk to me about how you are sorry you inconvenienced me." He turned around to walk away.

Sarah'd had just about enough. She ran to catch up to him, grabbing him by the arm and swinging him back around to face her.

"I *am* sorry. I'm sorry you ever had to deal with me showing up here. I never asked for you to come. I know I made a mistake, and I truly am sorry that you have to pay for it. There's nothing else I can say to let you know how sorry I am. But if you aren't going to be man enough to accept a sincere apology when it's given to you, then all I can say is that the one thing I'm most sorry about, is that I ever had the misfortune to meet you, Jake Montgomery."

With the words hanging in the air, Sarah turned her back on him, walking past her sister and mounting her horse as though she'd been doing it all her life. She kicked her heels into its sides and rode away, leaving both Jake and Beth standing in stunned silence.

She kept riding until she saw the familiar sight of her sister's ranch coming into view. Jake and Beth had caught up, but he'd hung back and let the women ride beside one another. As they came into the yard, they saw Ben and Everly standing on their porch waving. Everly held a little bundle in her arms, and Ben's two nieces were running toward them.

When they stopped, Jake rode alongside and threw one of the bags he'd been carrying with him to the ground. Not even dismounting, he said, "These ladies are all yours, Ben. I don't care if I don't see one hair on their pretty little heads for the rest of my days. They're your problem now, so I wish you luck."

With that, Sarah watched him ride further through the yard headed to his own house. She was sure if looks could kill, he would have fallen from his horse gasping for breath. She'd never been so angry in her life.

CHAPTER 6

"I've never met a more stubborn and pig-headed man in my life. I know I messed up by coming out here, and I tried more times than I care to remember to apologize for everything, but he won't even give me the chance. I didn't exactly get my dream wedding either, and if I'm being completely honest, I'm not even sure I'd want to be married to him anyway when he acts like this."

Sarah's pride was still stinging, and she knew even as she spoke she was sounding like a spoiled, ungrateful brat. But for some reason, when it came to Jake Montgomery, she just couldn't seem to keep her head straight.

She knew he'd done a lot to keep her safe and

she was grateful. She'd give anything she had to make things right, and to somehow try to fix everything, but he wouldn't even give her the time of day. She hadn't seen him since he dumped them on Everly's porch step over two days ago, and every day that passed gave her anger more time to grow.

"Sarah, you know that Jake saved you from a fate that could have ended quite badly for you," said Everly. "He didn't have to do it; he could have turned around and just rode away. In fact, he didn't even have to go out to meet your train in the first place. So you need to remember that everything he did to spare you ending up in the hands of a man who's obviously not at all trustworthy, was at a cost to him. Not only did he end up married, which is something he has clearly stated he did not ever want, but he also lost a stallion that was important to the future of his herd here at the ranch." Everly spoke to her exactly as she imagined her Momma would if she were here. Sarah could tell she was annoyed with her, and that made her feel like a child again.

She looked down at her hands as they crossed in her lap. "I know, Everly. I just hope that sometimes when I say the words, it'll help to ease the embarrassment and shame I feel over everything." She spoke quietly, as she stood up to lean against the post on Everly's front porch. She could see the men out in the pasture working with the horses, and her eyes seemed to find Jake's form automatically.

She continued, while her eyes followed Jake. "I never wanted any of this to happen. I know how badly I've messed everything up. I just didn't want to be a burden on Momma anymore, and I saw how happy you were with Ben...I guess, like always, I never thought things through before acting." She let her legs fold, and she sat down on the top step, wrapping her arms around her legs. She rested her chin on her knees.

She felt Everly's hand touch her shoulder, while Beth sat down beside her. "Sarah, the part that makes you special is the fact that when you decide to do something, there's nothing that will stop you. You are determined, and kind hearted, always believing only the best in everyone. So don't ever apologize for what you are." Even though Beth was the youngest sister, sometimes she just seemed to know what needed to be said.

"And why would you ever believe you'd be a

burden on Momma?" Everly asked as she came to sit on the other side of her.

Sarah looked toward Beth who just shrugged her shoulders. Realizing they'd never mentioned the conversation she'd overheard with their mother and Mr. McConnell, Sarah filled Everly in on everything she had heard, and how it'd made her decide she needed to let their Momma have her chance at a happy ending.

The girls sat quietly for awhile. They all wanted their mother to finally have someone to love and care for her like she deserved, so they understood Sarah's reasons for answering the ad to come west. Their momma had always put others before herself, and now it was her turn to be happy.

Finally Everly broke the silence. "You know, if you'd told me this from the beginning, you and Beth could have just said you wanted to come and live out here with me. You didn't need to risk so much by answering an ad like that."

Sarah was still watching Jake in the pasture. "I know. But you were newly married, with a baby on the way. You didn't need your little sisters coming out and getting in the way. Besides, I saw how wonderful everything turned out for you, and I hoped maybe I'd find the same thing." She let her gaze fall back down to her lap.

"But I guess my chances of that happening are over now."

The women hadn't heard Ben's young nieces come out onto the porch while they were talking. Olivia, who was now all grown up at eight years old, walked down the stairs and stood in front of Sarah.

"Do you love Uncle Jake?" she asked.

Sarah looked at this little girl standing before her, whom she'd grown to love, and smiled at the serious look on her face. Obviously, she'd heard enough of their conversation to feel like she should add her own thoughts.

"Well, Olivia, you know that love is a serious thing. And, sometimes it might not be enough anyway."

"But, do you love him?" Olivia wasn't backing down from her question, and as she stood standing in front of her, with her hands on her hips like she meant business, Sarah knew she wouldn't let it go until she answered truthfully.

"Yes, Olivia. I do love your Uncle Jake. I've loved him for a long time. But, one person loving the other isn't enough to make it work out. You can't force someone to love you back."

"How do you know he doesn't love you too? Uncle Jake is a very nice man, and I know he sure seems to look at you a lot when you're around him. I think he has a crush on you but maybe he doesn't know it."

Sarah couldn't help the blush that rose in her cheeks. "I'm pretty sure that your Uncle Jake is more annoyed with me than anything else."

"Have you ever told him you love him?" This time, Elizabeth asked the question.

Sarah sat staring at these young girls, unsure how they'd suddenly become so grown up. "Well no Elizabeth, I haven't ever really told him. It isn't that simple. You can't just tell someone you love them and expect them to love you back." She was trying to explain things to these girls that she wasn't even sure of herself.

"Why not?" Being just six years old, things seemed very simple in Elizabeth's eyes.

"Ya Sarah, why not?" Beth was grinning, as she was obviously enjoying Sarah's discomfort at this line of questioning. She shot her sister a glare, resisting the urge to stick her tongue out at her like she would have done when they were kids.

Everly was smiling as she stood up, taking the girl's hands. "Girls, Sarah and Uncle Jake have some things they need to work out on their own. Why don't you both run out to the garden and pick some peas for our supper tonight? And this time, try not to eat them all before you get back to the house." The girls ran off, giggling at the memory of the last time they'd picked peas and there hadn't been enough left for their meal.

"Everything seems so simple when you're a child." Sarah watched them running away, wishing she could have some of that innocence back.

"A lot of times, we make things harder for ourselves when we are adults. Maybe, it might be better to just let ourselves remember what we would have thought or done when we were children, without the worry of what might happen. Might not hurt for you to listen to what Olivia and Elizabeth were trying to say..." As Everly spoke, Sarah couldn't help but feel like it was her momma speaking to her.

She looked back up toward the pasture where the men were starting to head back to the barn. Her heart did the usual flutter when she saw Jake, and she realized that she truly did love him. When she'd said it to Olivia, it was the first time she'd actually ever said it out loud, and now that she had said it, she knew how true it was. She had to at least try to make things work with him.

She knew she'd never find another man she loved like him, even if he did make her so angry she wanted to scream. "You know what... I think it's time I started to push back a little bit to let my husband see that maybe he does have a bit of a crush on me too." She smiled at her sisters, as they both broke into wide grins seeing their sister back to her optimistic self.

"I really don't have anything to lose at this point anyway, do I?" She stood up, brushed the dust off her skirts, and headed into the house to start packing her bag up to head over to Jake's. After all, she was his wife whether he liked it or not.

It was time for her to show him that maybe he could like it, if he'd stop being so stubborn. She just hoped she wasn't about to make a bigger mess of things, if that were even possible.

"WOULD you mind telling me exactly what you think you're doing here?" Jake had walked in the door, tired and hungry from working all day with the horses. He normally would have stopped and ate with Ben and Everly, but knowing that Sarah was staying there had stopped him.

He hadn't expected to walk in the door of his own house and see her standing at the oven cooking. He looked around the house and noticed it had been cleaned as well. There were even flowers in a jar sitting on the table. The house was full of the smell of stew cooking, and his stomach betrayed him by starting to rumble.

"Well, I am your wife after all, so I figured it was time I came over here and started to do what a wife would do." He could tell she was nervous, even as she tried to sound like she had every right to be standing in that kitchen.

She still hadn't turned to look at him as she fussed at pouring the stew into a bowl. He noticed her splash a bit onto her finger, and then put it to her mouth to ease the pain of the burn. He couldn't help but wish he could just walk over and kiss her finger himself.

Shaking the thoughts from his head, he sat down at the chair by the table. He left his legs sprawled out, as he leaned back and crossed his arms over his chest.

"So, am I to gather that you also assume you'll be living here?" He raised an eyebrow toward her as she finally turned to bring the stew over to the table.

"That's what a wife would do, so I guess you assume correctly." He almost chuckled as he noticed her fighting to be nice, and not say what he was sure was really on her mind.

"And, where do you suppose then, that you'll be sleeping?" He had to catch the bowl of stew as she fumbled and started to drop it on the table in front of him as he asked the question. She looked at him with a horrified expression, which led him to believe she just realized that, once again, maybe she hadn't thought her plan all the way through.

"I'm not sure. But, I guess since I'm your wife, I should likely be sleeping where a wife would sleep." He noticed her swallow hard, lifting her chin higher while still not looking him in the eye. He had to admit he secretly admired her determination to try and act like she wasn't as shocked as she was obviously feeling.

He chuckled under his breath, and was sure that if he hadn't been feeling so hungry, and the food didn't smell so wonderful, he'd have been able to turn around and walk out the door. But, his stomach was begging him to just eat the food that was sitting in front of him. He pulled his chair up to the table and took a bite.

The stew was delicious, but he wasn't about to let her know that right away. "Tastes all right. You sure you didn't put any poison in it, or anything else I should be worried about?" He lifted an eyebrow while he looked at her, and had to laugh again at the genuine look of shock on her face as she finally met his gaze.

"I assure you I didn't. Although I'd be lying if I said I didn't think about it." She turned her back to him, finally realizing he was just trying to start an argument. She poured herself a bowl, and sat down to eat. He noticed she was only picking at her food, sensing that she was uneasy sitting across from him.

"You never answered my question about why you suddenly felt the need to show up here and play the role of wife. I made it clear that we're married in the eyes of the law, but that's as far as it goes." He knew he was being a brute, but he was not ready to just let her waltz in here and be his wife. He'd lived too long with bitterness eating him up to just be able to let it go.

The fact that it wasn't her fault he felt that way

didn't change his mind one bit. She was still a woman, and he was pretty sure they were all the same.

She looked him in the eye without wavering, causing him to squirm uncomfortably. "I received some advice today from some very wise ladies. I know I have a lot of work to do to prove to you that I can be a good wife. Maybe I never will, but I have to at least try. I know what you sacrificed to keep me safe when we were in Mulder Creek, and I owe it to you to at least try and make things up to you. Whether or not I can will remain up to you."

She put her eyes back down and took a bite.

"Just like a woman to think everything can be worked out as though nothing ever happened." He mumbled under his breath, without realizing she'd been able to hear him.

She stood up, putting her arms on her hips. "Listen, Jake Montgomery, I don't know why you have such anger towards women, or what has caused you to be so completely against marriage, but I assure you, I won't be just walking away to let you spend the rest of your days sulking here like a spoiled child who didn't get their way one time. I intend to at least try, so you can be as big an oaf as you like. I can see past that, and intend to show you that sometimes you just have to trust your heart." She was shaking as she turned her back to him.

"You can do whatever you like to try and change my mind," Jake said. "But I promise you, I'll not be made a fool of. So if you have any intentions of trying to wrangle your way into my life, you're wasting your time. I have learned firsthand what happens when you trust your heart, and I think it's time you learned that sometimes your heart is wrong."

He pushed himself away from the table, and stormed out the door. He headed to the stables and as far away from Sarah as he could get. He knew he'd hurt her. He'd seen the pain flash in her eyes when she turned to face him while he spoke, and he hoped she'd be smart enough to pack up her things and head back to Ben's. She didn't belong with him.

So why did his heart hold a tiny sliver of hope that she'd still be there when he came back?

CHAPTER 7

*M*ore than a week had passed, and Sarah still wasn't feeling any closer to breaking down the walls around Jake than she was when she got there. Even after that first night when he'd walked out, she had stayed, determined to somehow make things work.

She wasn't so sure anymore she was doing the right thing.

"So, if you don't mind me asking, since you don't seem willing to fill me in, how are things with you and Jake? He doesn't seem as angry as he was, but he still seems like he's going out of his way to make you dislike him." Beth was chewing on an apple as they knelt on the ground watching the kids play on the banks by the creek.

They had just left church, and were setting out a blanket with a picnic lunch at Olivia and Elizabeth's request. They loved the Sundays when everyone stopped for a picnic, and they had asked their Uncle Jake yesterday if he'd join them. Unable to ever say no to them, he had agreed, even when they'd insisted he had to bring "Aunt" Sarah, as they were already calling her.

"Well, it's been a long week. He spends as much time away from the house as he possibly can, and when he does come home to eat and sleep, he makes sure to be as ornery as he can towards me. I've cleaned his house top to bottom, cooked meals that most people would be thrilled to be served, mended holes in socks that would've been better used as rags, and tried to make his house a home." She snapped the blanket fiercely as she spoke, causing Everly to look over with a questioning look.

"I take it he isn't being appreciative of any of it?" Beth was trying to grab hold of the other side of the blanket, but Sarah seemed not to notice.

"I even offered to be his wife, completely." By now, Everly had walked over to see what was causing the delay in getting the picnic set up. She raised her eyebrows as Sarah blushed. Beth sat with her mouth hanging open.

"What did he say?" Beth looked horrified.

"He turned his back on me. I put myself out there, offering the only thing I felt I could to show him how I truly felt. And he walked away to go sleep back in the barn where he's been sleeping since I showed up. I've never been so humiliated in my life." Tears had started to well in her eyes as she spoke. She quickly looked down, patting at wrinkles that weren't really there in the blanket.

"I don't know how much more I can take. He's decided he doesn't want to be married, and I did my best to try making things right. I guess if I truly do care about him, it's time to give him what he wants. It isn't fair to keep forcing this on him. He saved me from getting hurt, or worse, at the hands of Hank Barlow. Now it's my turn to pay him back." She looked up to where he was swinging Elizabeth in the air.

Somehow, sensing her eyes on him, he turned and looked at her. Wishing she could turn her eyes away before he noticed the tears, she watched as he set the girl on the ground. He quickly shook his head as though trying to clear his thoughts, then turned and grabbed Olivia and gave her a turn.

Putting on a brave smile, she looked at her sisters. "What are you going to do?" Everly asked.

"Something I should have done from the first day we got back to High Ridge." She'd already decided what she needed to do. Now, she needed to convince her stepbrother Andrew to help her. He was the only man she could trust to not tell Jake.

She saw him standing by the wagon talking to Ben. She stood up and walked over to him. "Can I talk to you, Andrew? It will just be a minute." Understanding she wanted to speak to him alone, Ben walked over to the ladies on the blanket. Sarah watched him bend down and kiss Everly softly on the cheek as he sat down beside her. Her heart ached for a love like that.

She needed to be strong enough to go through with her plan, and not let her hopes and her feelings for Jake get in the way.

"What can I do for you, sis?" Andrew light-heartedly asked. Even though they'd never been raised together, and he wasn't related by blood, he'd taken on the duty of big brother towards all three sisters.

Their father had been married to Andrew's mother Lucy, who'd been widowed at a young age after Andrew was born. Her father had been forced into an acceptable marriage with Andrew's mother to save his family's fortune, but he'd also continued his relationship with Sarah's mother.

Lucy had known about the other family her husband had, and Sarah knew it had to have been painful for her to live with. Lucy had been angry after Thomas died, and had tried to ruin Everly's chance at marriage. Things had been quite rocky between all of them, and there were still a lot of unresolved feelings about those years.

But, Andrew had never been anything but kind to the three of them, never blaming them for any of the circumstances that had ruled the lives of their parents, and they all looked upon him now as a true brother.

"I was hoping you could take me into town with you the next time you go. I have a few errands to run."

He looked at her suspiciously. Even though he hadn't known her his whole life, he was already able to tell when she was up to something.

"And is there a reason your husband can't take you?" He was watching her closely, and she didn't want to give anything away. He knew things weren't perfect between her and Jake, and he knew the circumstances that had led to their marriage. But, he also had assumed since she was now living out there with him that everything had worked out in her favor.

"No, I don't want to bother him. I know he's busy. I was hoping to surprise him with a gift." She was having a hard time keeping eye contact, and she sensed that he didn't quite believe her.

"Well, I have to head in to town in the morning. I suppose I could let you tag along." He didn't sound convinced, but at least he wasn't saying no. "But we should tell Jake. We wouldn't want him worrying if he came home and you weren't there."

"Oh, don't worry. I'll tell him. I'll just mention that I need some supplies, and he won't mind me going as long as you're taking me." She turned abruptly to get away before he changed his mind, not realizing Jake had walked up behind her. She ran right into his chest, almost falling backwards before his arms reached out to grab her waist.

"And where exactly are you planning on going?" He was still holding her, and she was having trouble getting her thoughts together in her head. She hadn't intended to tell him anything, so she was trying to think of what she could say without looking suspicious.

"I'm just going to go in to town with Andrew tomorrow for a ride. I would like to get out of the house a bit and we need a few supplies. I didn't want to bother you to take me because I know how busy you are, and I was going to ask you first to make sure it was all right...." She was trying to pull herself free from his grip before her legs gave out and she ended up swooning in his arms like some love sick little girl.

She needed to stay strong enough to do what she'd decided to do. And standing here in his arms, looking in those eyes that melted her heart, was not going to work in her favor.

He chuckled low in his throat as he let her free. "You're free to go wherever you choose, ma'am." As he spoke, he tipped his hat down in her direction then turned and walked away.

If she wasn't such a lady, she'd be searching the ground for a rock to throw at his head. Instead, she lifted her chin and walked back to the blanket where the others were pretending to not have seen the exchange.

She put on the biggest smile she could, and sat down as though nothing had happened. But inside, her stomach was in knots and she felt like her world was crashing around her. After she went to town tomorrow, there'd be no turning back. And, even though she knew she had to do it, it didn't stop her heart from breaking in pieces.

JAKE STORMED AWAY. He wasn't sure why he was so annoyed at Sarah asking Andrew to take her to town, but he was. He knew he hadn't been very nice to her the past few days, so he really couldn't be surprised that she'd ask someone else.

He wondered what she was going to town for. She said she needed supplies, but for some reason, he felt there was more to it. She hadn't been able to look him in the eye, and she seemed nervous when he'd walked over. He looked back where she was sitting on the blanket with the others.

Everyone was laughing and seemed to be having a good time. It irritated him to see her laughing and having so much fun with everyone else. Yet, he hadn't given her anything to laugh about, so why he even cared caused him to be even angrier with himself.

"Are you going to stand there scowling and moping all day, or do you think you might join the rest of us and try to enjoy yourself a bit?" Ben had walked over to where he was pretending to tend to the horses. "Pretty sure the horses are all taken care of and will enjoy the rest." He was smirking, which didn't help Jake's mood.

"You know, it's a funny thing when a woman gets under your skin. You kind of feel like you're losing control of your life, and suddenly everything they do matters to you." He was still grinning, but Jake wasn't ready to let go of his bad mood just yet.

"Well, you're right about one thing. That woman has got under my skin, but not in a good way. She's made more of a mess in the short time she's been here than anyone else has ever managed to do in my entire life. She seems to think we would be well suited in this marriage I was forced into, but the truth is, we make each other so angry when we're together I can't see how it would ever work out the way she imagines." He was brushing his horse so vigorously it was starting to whinny loudly.

"And, there's the fact that, thanks to her, I lost the stallion I'd worked for a long time getting; the one that was going to make our ranch known as the best around these parts. Or, have you forgotten that part?" He looked at Ben with a raised eyebrow.

That stallion was just as important to Ben, and he couldn't understand how he didn't seem angry about it one bit.

"No, I haven't forgotten about Atlas. However, I also know that Sarah is someone very important to the woman I love, which makes her important to me. I've known her long enough to know that she'd never have done anything like this on purpose. Her only fault was being too trusting." Ben walked over and took the brush out of Jake's hand before the horse had no hide left.

"She didn't come out here to cause you harm. Everly told me she'd been quite hurt when she left here after our marriage. She had hoped for more from a man she'd grown to care for while she was here, but that man didn't want anything more from her. And, she was only coming out here, answering an ad for marriage to a stranger, because she overheard her mother talking to Alistair McConnell about not being able to marry him until her daughters were all settled and happy." He stopped talking until Jake finally looked at him.

"The only reason she even came out here was so her mother would be free to marry, and have her happy ending that Sarah felt she deserved. She wasn't even doing it for herself."

Jake looked over at the women. Sarah was playing with Ben's nieces, covering her eyes while the girls ran off to hide. They were all giggling and he secretly wished he could join in the fun.

"If you would've ever taken a few moments to talk to her, you would have realized that she was never coming out here with the intention of hurting you or causing you any trouble. She was thrown into this just as much as you were, and she has tried everything to make it up to you. But you're being stubborn and fool-headed about it all, taking it out on her for something she had no part in ever wanting to have caused in the first place."

Jake looked at his cousin as he noticed how angry he was beginning to sound. Ben wasn't the type to get mad over a lot of things, but when he did, he always had good reason. He looked back toward the people sitting on the blanket and saw Sarah watching him. She blushed when his eyes met hers, and he finally let himself admit that she was just about the most beautiful woman he'd ever met.

He turned and smiled at Ben. "Well, I never thought I'd see the day when Ben Montgomery would be giving me advice about women."

Ben thumped him on the back as they started

to walk toward the blanket. "Trust me, Jake. Understanding women is just about the hardest thing you and I will ever do. But, sometimes when you look at them, and feel something you never really thought you'd ever feel for another person, none of that matters. All that matters is seeing them smile."

Realizing he was starting to sound like a lovesick sap, he cleared his throat. "And besides, life is just a whole lot simpler when they are happy."

They laughed as they joined the rest of the group. Olivia grabbed Jake's hand. "Come play hide and seek with us, Uncle Jake!" She pulled him with her, leaving him no choice.

He noticed the smile on Sarah's face before he was dragged away, and he thought how true Ben's words were. Seeing her smile did warm his heart, and that thought scared him more than he cared to admit.

CHAPTER 8

"*Y*ou may as well tell me what you're doing, Sarah. I'm not going to stop asking until I find out." Andrew was driving the wagon with Sarah and Beth sitting up on the bench beside him. He'd chosen to take the wagon knowing the women were going in with him, and he had said he could use it to bring back more supplies he needed.

Sarah sighed. He'd been trying to find out why she was going in to town ever since she'd asked him yesterday. He knew she was up to something, and he wasn't letting it go.

"Andrew, if I tell you, you have to promise me that you won't be heading straight back to Jake and telling him anything." She pinned her gaze on him

81

until he started squirming, saying he wouldn't say a word to anyone.

"You know the circumstances of my marriage to Jake. He wasn't exactly happy about what happened, being forced into a marriage to someone he never wanted. Not to mention losing his prize stallion." She added the last words quietly, while putting her head down to look at the hands in her lap.

"I've tried to make things right with him, but he'll never be happy with how things have worked out. I don't want to make him suffer any more for a situation he had no control over. He saved me from ending up with someone who could have done serious harm to me, and now I have to let him off the hook for what he did." She watched Andrew's face to see his reaction.

She could tell he was trying to understand what she was getting at, and knew the moment he finally figured it out. He snapped his head towards her. "You mean you're leaving him? Just like that?" He sounded horrified.

"No, that isn't what I'm doing, Andrew! You should know by now that's not the kind of person I am. I'm sending a wire to Mr. McConnell asking him to draw up papers for an annulment." She blushed as she realized now Andrew would likely be able to figure out that nothing had happened between her and Jake which would have prevented the marriage being annulled.

Before he could question it, she continued. "I'm also going to ask for all of the money from my trust left to me from my father. I know each of us received large sums after Everly went through with her marriage, as he'd stipulated in his will. I intend to find out from Hank Barlow what it will cost to get Jake's horse back, and I'm going to make sure he gets it."

She kept her eyes straight ahead, and she knew both Andrew and her sister were looking at her. This was the first Beth had heard about her plan too, and she was bracing for the arguments from both of them. When things remained quiet, she looked over to Beth. She was staring at her with a look she didn't recognize.

"Well, aren't you going to tell me what a horrible mistake I'm making?" She turned her head to Andrew. "And I'm sure you likely have some-thing to say!" She couldn't believe neither of them was saying anything to her.

"You're a grown woman, Sarah. You don't need my approval one way or another." Andrew wasn't even looking at her, keeping his eyes straight ahead.

"Besides, it's not like you'd listen to what we say anyway. Sounds like you've already made your decision. And we all know once you decide on something, nothing anyone says would change your mind." Beth was still looking at her strangely. "But, did you ever ask Jake what he thought about an annulment? Or if he even cared if he got his horse back? I know I've never even heard him mention it since the day he picked us up in Mulder Creek. Almost seems like you are the only one still bothered by it."

Sarah just stared at Beth. Her little sister hadn't always agreed with her, and when she didn't, she usually came out with both guns blazing to point out why she thought Sarah was wrong. This time though, she seemed to be very calm about it all as she asked questions Sarah wasn't sure she wanted to answer.

"Just because he hasn't said anything, doesn't mean it isn't still bothering him. You've both seen how he acts around me. He's made it clear I'm not what he wanted in his life. And, if I can get his horse back, and give him his freedom back, at least I can move on with my life without enduring the guilt I feel at ruining his." She clenched her teeth together as she spoke, unsure how either Beth or Andrew could think this wasn't the best thing for everyone involved.

She saw the other two share a look, sensing she was done talking about it. She was glad they decided to let it go for now, even though knowing them both as she did, she was sure they'd still have more to say. She didn't need them causing her to have any more doubts than she already was having -- especially after the picnic yesterday.

After he overheard her saying she was going into town, he'd stomped off to tend to the horses. But, he'd eventually come over and joined everyone else. She thought he'd even let his guard down a little bit to have some fun.

She'd enjoyed watching him play with Olivia and Elizabeth. They'd dragged him all over, and he hadn't complained once. He'd sat on the blanket while everyone ate, laughing and relaxing enough to truly enjoy the day with the family.

Secretly, Sarah had let herself imagine they were a happy couple, enjoying a wonderful day with everyone. He'd even been civil with her, which had surprised her. He hadn't gone out of his way to be nice to her since the day he'd dragged her here.

After they'd returned home, she had made a wonderful supper and they'd actually sat down and spent a nice evening together talking. But, he was still guarded around her, and she suspected the good mood wouldn't last. She'd realized how much she wanted to let him be happy, and if that meant giving him his freedom back, she knew she had to go through with her plan.

As she replayed yesterday in her mind, she noticed the sight of High Ridge coming into her view. She swallowed hard as she tried to convince her heart she was still doing the right thing.

JAKE PULLED on the reins as he neared High Ridge. He wasn't sure why he'd felt the need to come into town today, other than hoping to see what Sarah was doing. They'd left earlier when he was out working in the pasture with the horses, but he knew Andrew had decided to take the wagon, which would have slowed their trip down.

He was annoyed with himself for even caring what she was doing in town. He tried to hide the fact by pretending he was just making sure she wasn't up to something that would cause him any more grief.

He still wasn't sure what he'd say when he saw them, but he figured he would come up with something by then. He could pretend he was collecting the mail or paying a bill. There was no way he'd let her know he was actually worried about her safety with men like the Barlow's skulking around town, or that he was suspicious she was up to something that affected him.

Andrew would protect her with his life; he had no doubt about that. But, he still felt that he had to offer his protection as well. He knew he wouldn't have been able to concentrate anyway while she was gone.

He spotted the wagon right away, hitched in front of the mercantile. He cringed knowing he'd have to see the meddling old woman who ran the store, Hazel Hayes. She'd tried unsuccessfully to force Ben into marrying her daughter, almost causing him to lose care of his nieces and his chance of marrying Everly. He hated the woman intensely, but he was forced to deal with her as she owned the only mercantile in town.

As he pulled alongside the wagon, he noticed

Sarah coming from the telegraph office just up the street. The man who put out the newspaper for this whole area had an office there, where he also ran the telegraph.

Jake watched as Sarah walked toward the wagon. He still sat on his horse, with his arms crossed on the saddle horn. He knew the exact moment she saw him, as her steps fumbled. She stopped walking and stood staring at him with a look of shock. He kept his eyes on her, with his eyebrows raised. He was asking her a question without speaking, and he knew she wasn't happy to see him.

"What are you doing in town, Jake? You never mentioned you were coming in today as well." She was trying to sound like she wasn't rattled at seeing him, but she wasn't fooling him. He dismounted from his horse, leading him closer to where she was standing.

"You don't sound happy to see your husband. I had my own reasons for coming to town today, which if you'd ever asked me, I would've been more than happy to have you accompany me for the ride." He was enjoying watching her squirm, and wondered why she kept glancing across the street towards the sheriff's office. He looked over and saw Beth coming out the door with the sheriff.

Since High Ridge was close enough to Mulder Creek, not to mention the fact that it wasn't a job many people wanted, Sheriff Dixon spent his time working both places. Jake wasn't surprised to see it was the same man who'd married him and Sarah.

They both stopped when they saw him, and he noticed Beth say something to him, then run across to them. The sheriff just stood there watching her, and he was almost positive he noticed the man give a slight shake of his head as though he was completely dumbfounded by the woman he was watching cross the street. He looked at Jake, giving a slight tug on his hat in greeting before turning to go back in his office.

If he'd ever wondered whether or not they were up to something, now he had no doubt in his mind.

"Want to tell me what's going on, or should I head over to Sheriff Dixon and ask myself? I might even have to make a stop at the telegraph office to see what business you might have had in there." He was starting to get angry. If she was up to something, she better come clean now.

"Jake, there's nothing for you to worry about.

All I was doing at the telegraph office was sending a message to Momma to tell her we're all doing all right. And, I'd asked Beth to ask the sheriff if he thought Hank Barlow was going to cause us any more trouble. Nothing you need to worry about." She was talking fast, and he doubted she was telling him the truth. But, just then, he noticed someone walking toward them that stopped any further questioning. Bracing for a confrontation, he moved closer to Sarah.

"Jake! Oh my goodness! You're a sight for sore eyes. I'm so happy to see you!" He barely had time to register what was happening before the slight woman threw herself into his arms. "How are you doing? I've missed you so much. I heard a terrible rumor that you'd got yourself married, but I know it can't be true. Please, tell me it isn't true!"

Pulling her arms from around his shoulders, now it was his turn to squirm as he noticed the look of fury on Sarah's face.

Setting the woman away from him, he reached over and pulled Sarah closer to him. "Anna, I'd like you to meet my wife, Sarah. Sarah, this is Anna." He wished at this moment he'd decided to stay home. He could feel the tension in Sarah's body as he held her next to him.

Anna's mouth gaped open briefly before she remembered her manners. However, she couldn't hide her look of anger as she looked at Sarah. He noticed Sarah looked like she was ready to scratch the other woman's eyes out, so he decided to keep a tight grip on her waist.

"So it *is* true," She looked at Jake and put her mouth into a pout. As he watched her try to manipulate him, he wondered what he'd ever thought he loved about her. "Is it also true you were forced into the marriage? I heard rumors that your new wife had actually come out here to marry Hank Barlow, but you being the good man you are, stepped in to save her from that horrible fate." She was giving Sarah a snide smirk as she said the words.

"Not sure who you're hearing all the rumors from, but I assure you, my marriage to Sarah is real. The circumstances of how it happened are nobody's business but mine." He wished Andrew would hurry up and get back from wherever he was, because he could feel that both Sarah and Beth were just about ready to cause even more of a scene.

"Did you ever tell your new wife about me?" She was looking at Jake, and then turned her gaze back to Sarah. "Did he ever tell you about our past? We were together for the longest time, and were to be married. I made a horrible mistake, falling for lies from Hank Barlow; much like you did I hear. Jake and I were working on fixing our relationship so we could be married. Rumor is that he only married you to get even with Hank -- stealing the woman he was supposed to marry the same way Hank did to him by stealing me away." She looked back to Jake. "I know you still love me, Jake. There's no way you could just forget our history together. I'll wait for you to come to your senses and realize you don't need to stay married to someone you were forced to wed."

With those words, she started to turn to leave. Jake was completely dumbfounded and unable to speak as he listened to the words Anna was saying. Thankfully, he was spared having to say anything by Sarah who was obviously having no trouble finding her voice.

"He may have been forced to marry me, but I'd think by the manner you are speaking to me in public that he's been spared a fate worse than death by not getting stuck with the likes of you. You're a vile, angry woman and I know that Jake would've been miserable had he ever been left to spend the rest of his days with you. I pray that no matter what happens in his future, he will never, ever be subjected to a life with someone as bitter and horrible as you." Sarah was shaking, holding her hands in fists at her sides. Jake was sure he'd never seen her this angry.

As Anna stood on the spot, looking like she'd just been slapped, Andrew finally came out of the store. Unaware of what had just happened, he was whistling as he came around the wagon, dumping a bag of feed into the back. "Jake! What are you doing in town?" He waited for a response, and then sensed that something had just transpired between the people standing in the street.

"Come on, Andrew. Let's get going." Sarah turned her back on Anna, walking around to the side of the wagon. Beth glared at the other woman, and then went around with her sister. Raising his eyebrows, Andrew looked at Jake for some answers.

"Well, that's quite the wife you have there, Jake. I wish you both nothing but happy years ahead." Speaking through clenched teeth, there was no question her words were not sincere. Anna turned and walked away, leaving Jake standing there with Andrew staring at him waiting for an explanation.

Not ready to get into anything with the other man, he walked over and grabbed Sarah by the wrist as she started to climb into the wagon. "You'll be riding home with me. And next time you decide to go running off into town, you'll ask your husband to take you."

CHAPTER 9

*S*arah sat in front of Jake on the horse as they rode home. She made sure she kept her back as stiff as she could so she wouldn't accidentally brush against him. He'd dragged her rather unceremoniously from where she was starting to climb into the wagon and practically thrown her on his horse. Before she'd even had a chance to argue, he had turned his horse and was galloping away from town.

She could only imagine what Andrew and Beth would be thinking as they followed behind in the wagon.

Jake seemed committed to making her angry at every turn. It was almost as though he was trying to make her hate him. After his performance today, she was so glad she'd decided to go through with sending for annulment papers. He really was a brute of a man, and now that she saw the kind of woman he was truly attracted to, she was glad to be getting free of him.

She tried to convince herself the truth in her words as they rode in silence.

"You'll have a mighty sore back if you stay that rigid all the way back to the ranch." He seemed to be taunting her, knowing how angry she was, to relax and lean herself into him. She wouldn't give him the satisfaction.

"I'm fine. I can live with a sore back." She didn't care if her spine broke in half, she'd sit like this the rest of the way home.

"Suit yourself." He kicked his heels into the horse, taking off at a faster pace. She had no choice but to lean back or she would've surely been on the ground in a heap.

She was sure she could sense his lips moving into a grin, and she wished she could turn around and slap the smile right off his face. Instead, she focused on hanging on for her life as he kept the horse going as fast as he could.

After they got far enough ahead of the others, he slowed the horse back down. She was lost in her thoughts so didn't even notice she could have sat back up again.

How could Jake have possibly ever had feelings for a woman like Anna? She couldn't understand how someone she'd come to know as honorable and kind, even if he didn't show it to her, would fall in love with someone so hateful?

Perhaps she hadn't always been like that, and losing Jake had caused her to become bitter. She just didn't think anyone could change that much.

The part that stung the most, if she was completely honest with herself, was the fact that he could love someone so spiteful and mean, yet not let himself care for someone like her. What was wrong with her that he couldn't bring himself to fall in love with her?

She tried not to let her thoughts consume her, but as they rode in silence, she couldn't think of anything else. She felt even worse knowing he'd been in love with someone else, and because of her, he'd lost his chances with Anna. Even if she wasn't someone Sarah thought would be good to him, it wasn't her place to decide. No wonder he was still so angry with her. His marriage to her had cost him his true love.

What she couldn't figure out was why he didn't

just let her leave with Andrew and Beth. He could've talked to Anna and tried to explain. One thing she was beginning to understand about Jake Montgomery was that he didn't make sense.

"So, aren't you going to ask me about Anna? I imagine you're full of questions. I know what you're like Sarah, and I'm pretty sure you're just about bursting wanting to know about her." She stiffened her back again as she realized she'd still been leaning into his chest. She could feel the vibration when he started to speak, pulling her out of her thoughts.

He wasn't letting her go that easy though, and pulled her back closer before she could get fully upright. "You know Sarah, I won't bite." She could sense that grin again and it fueled her anger. How could he be so untroubled about everything that had happened back there?

"What happened between you and Anna is none of my concern. I may be your wife in name and on paper, but that is as far as it goes. I don't pretend to be any more than that, as you've been sure to make very clear to me. I'm glad you were at least able to get some satisfaction from marrying the woman Hank was supposed to be marrying." She tried to control her voice, but couldn't help notice how her voice cracked at the end as she fought to maintain her composure.

Why did she even care? The part that bothered her most was that she did care. She cared more than she wanted to admit. She knew she had to get that annulment done, and get as far away from him as she could. Her heart would mend in time, but she knew she had to get away. She could go back to Chicago. Hopefully by now, her momma would have realized she loved Mr. McConnell and would go ahead and marry him regardless of what her daughters were doing.

"Anna was a gold digger, and I was a foolish young man. Hank Barlow saved me from marrying someone I would've been miserable with for the rest of my life. And, regardless of what others may be saying, I never married you to get back at Hank. I married you to keep you safe from him." With that, she realized he was done explaining.

He kicked his heels in again, and they raced home. He kept his arms tight around her waist, and she couldn't help the tears that finally broke free. She felt so safe in his arms, yet she knew it wasn't real. The only person she needed saving from was the one who was holding her in his arms.

SHE LOOKED down into the bluest eyes she'd ever seen, and wondered how someone so tiny could have worked their way into her heart so easily. Everly's baby boy, Thomas, cooed and smiled up at his aunt, causing Sarah to pull him up to her face for a kiss.

"He sure does love you." Everly smiled as she looked over at her.

"Well, his Auntie Sarah loves him just as much." She scrunched her face up as Thomas touched her cheek.

"I wasn't talking about Thomas." Sarah's eyes shot toward her sister. Everly was sitting mending a shirt while they sat on the front porch. The day had been hot, and they were cooling down before the men came back from checking the cattle in the far pasture. Her sister never even raised her eyes from her mending.

"Do you mind explaining who you're referring to then, Everly?" She was looking at her sister with a raised eyebrow, waiting for her to finish. Beth was helping the girls take some of the laundry off the line, so it was just the two of them.

"I've seen the way he looks at you, Sarah, when

you aren't watching. And, you have to admit, these past few days he hasn't been as ornery towards you as he was when you first came here." She smiled as she looked at Sarah.

"If I didn't know better, I'd say he is perhaps letting himself accept the fact that he's now a married man, to a woman he might possibly have feelings for."

Sarah stared at her sister incredulous. "You can't be serious?" While things had been more civil between the two of them since they got back from town, she didn't know if she could agree with how her sister saw things. He still seemed to enjoy baiting her into arguing with him, and he hadn't exactly been loving towards her.

He still stayed away as much as he could, but she did admit that when he came home, he was at least trying to get along with her.

But that was as far as it had gone. He still slept in the barn, and only spent time in the house with her during meals. The rest of the time, he left her alone.

That wasn't exactly how she saw a loving couple to be spending their days together.

She was ready to explain all of that to her sister when they heard a yell from the pasture as the men were racing up to the house. They stood up, rushing down the steps to meet them. Sarah was still holding Thomas so she wasn't able to run as fast as Everly.

"What's going on?" Everly was the first to shout.

"Rustlers! They've taken over half our herd from the far pasture. Looks like they have at least a day's ride ahead of us, so we need to get going so we can catch up to them. We'll be taking Andrew and a couple of the other men, but we'll leave two or three hands here to help out in case we are gone for long." Ben was down from his horse, taking Everly in his arms. She was scared, and it showed on her face.

"What? You can't just leave like that! Don't you need to take supplies with you, some food, anything?" Sarah was standing there shocked, and sensing her tension, Thomas started to fuss. Ben came over and took him from her arms. She noticed how lovingly he looked at his son as he carried him gently in his arms back over to Everly.

She looked at Jake, unsure what to do. "We'll gather a few supplies from the barn before we head out." He was watching her intently.

"Well, we have stew made fresh in the house,

just let me go and get you all some to at least take with you!" She went to turn and go in the house. He hopped off his horse and grabbed her arm, stopping her.

By now, Beth had run over to see what was happening. "The girls and I can get it ready for them, Sarah." She took the girls' hands and raced into the house. Sensing something was very wrong, the girls didn't argue.

Jake was still staring at her, and Sarah felt herself being pulled toward him. His lips came down on hers so gently she thought her legs would give out beneath her. Thankfully, he had his arms around her waist and held her close so she didn't fall. He'd kissed her on their wedding day, but this was a different kiss. This one was beautifully tender. She felt her own arms go up around his neck, and she was sure he groaned as he kissed her even deeper.

He pulled back as they heard the screen door slam. The girls were running down the stairs, oblivious to the goodbyes that were taking place in the yard. Everyone knew that going after rustlers could end badly. Rustlers in these parts were known to be dangerous, and when they had a good payout like the cattle they'd just stolen, they weren't apt to let them go without a fight.

Sarah looked at Jake, trying to get the words out that she desperately wanted to say. She wanted to say not to go, that she was sorry -- anything she could to make him stay. But, she knew he wouldn't. All she could whisper was, "Please, be careful."

He smiled, lifted his hand to her cheek and nodded. Just then, Olivia launched herself into his arms. "Uncle Jake, be careful! I don't want you or Uncle Ben to get hurt!" She had tears in her eyes, and Sarah noticed Elizabeth was now in Ben's arms.

Without taking his eyes off Sarah's, Jake offered reassurance to Olivia as he hugged her close. "Don't you worry about me, sweetheart. I'll be careful." Sarah was sure he was saying the words to her.

"Besides, I have an awful lot to come back for."

Taking the food that Beth was holding out for them, the men hopped back on their horses and headed for the barn. Sarah couldn't take her eyes off Jake, and she could feel her legs starting to give out. Luckily, Beth was there to hold her up.

She looked toward Everly and noticed she

looked the same way she felt as she was watching Ben's disappearing back. They walked over to her, and the sisters, along with Olivia and Elizabeth, held each other while they tried not to let their thoughts cause too much worry.

They waited until they saw them leave the barn. Jake looked over and their eyes met. He pulled his hat down, spun his horse and raced down the road with the others.

"Do you have any doubt left now about how that man feels about you, Sarah?" Everly was trying to lighten the mood, but Sarah was feeling too heartsick to respond.

She'd just realized the man she loved might actually care for her too. And, as she watched him ride away, she didn't know if she'd ever have the chance to tell him how she truly felt.

CHAPTER 10

Sarah sat in the big chair by the window, looking out at the sprawling land for as far as she could see. It truly was beautiful here, and she had to admit she felt more at home here than she ever had in Chicago. She could hear birds in the trees, in the distance she could hear mother cows calling to their calves, and the whinnying of the horses in the pasture just beside the house.

It'd been almost two days since Jake and Ben had rode away. She was sure they had to have caught up to the rustlers by now, and it scared her to think of what the outcome had been. She'd heard enough since she came out here to know how dangerous cattle rustlers could be.

She got up from the chair before her thoughts

could get away on her. She'd cleaned every square inch of the house, every window was sparkling, and every bit of laundry had been washed, dried and folded. She'd been baking to pass the time as she waited desperately for word of the men.

She'd gone to Everly's yesterday and would head back today. Being alone with her thoughts was dangerous.

But each night since Jake left, she'd come home, wrapped herself in the one shirt she hadn't let herself wash, and fell asleep with his scent around her. Sleep had eluded her, as she laid awake thinking and praying until the early morning hours.

As she was getting her shawl to wrap around her shoulders for the walk to Everly's, she thought she heard shouting from outside. Running to the door, she flew outside to see horses racing towards the house. She could see Jake's horse running behind, but he wasn't in the saddle. Her hand flew to her throat as she screamed, running out to meet the horses that were coming towards her.

Finally, she saw two men on Ben's horse and she realized that one of them was Jake. Crying now with relief, she almost fell to the ground, until she noticed that Jake was slumped in the saddle in front of Ben.

"Jake's been shot, Sarah. We need to get him into the house and get the doctor here right away!" Ben sounded like he was just as scared as she was, as he looked her in the eye begging her to help him take care of him.

"Here, let me help you get him in the house." She started to walk to the horse. Hearing her voice, he mumbled that he was perfectly fine to get himself in the house. Ben jumped off the horse, and Jake put his leg out to dismount.

In obvious pain, he crumpled to the ground and Sarah raced over to him. She could see blood puddling under his leg where he was gripping it in agony. "Don't be such a stubborn oaf, Jake!" She knelt down, putting his arm around her shoulders. Ben was doing the same on the other side, and together they stood and helped him into the house.

They carried him to the bed and helped him lay down. Ben, understanding the nature of the relationship between the two of them, and unsure how much Sarah would be willing to help, told her to leave the room while he helped Jake get his pants off so he could clean the wound out.

"Absolutely not, Ben! I'm still his wife, and I'm perfectly capable of helping you tend to his wound. I assure you, I won't faint at the sight of bare skin or a bleeding wound." With that, she grabbed onto one pant leg while Ben pulled on the other.

The pain got to be too much, and thankfully Jake passed out. Seeing him so vulnerable, and so hurt, tore at Sarah's heart. She knew she'd never felt fear like she did at this moment, but she also knew she had to hold herself together and help him.

She wouldn't even let herself think the worst. Her soul couldn't bare the pain.

They got him undressed, and she ran to boil some water on the stove. Her hands were fumbling, causing her to drop the pot onto the floor. She bent down to pick it up and realized she was having difficulty seeing. Ben's hand reached out to pick the pot up, and his other came out to help her stand.

By now, the tears were flowing freely while she took the pot from him, filled it with water and stoked the fire to get it to boil. She was desperately trying to think of anything else she could do to try and help Jake, but instead she just stood there wringing her hands and staring at Ben with fear in her eyes.

"He'll be alright, Sarah. The bullet just went into his leg. He's a tough, stubborn old goat so it'll take more than a bullet to slow him down." Ben tried to smile at her with his reassurance, but she could see the fear in his eyes as well.

One of the cow hands who'd gone with them had rode ahead to tell Everly what had happened, while another had rode into town to get the doctor. Everly came racing through the door, throwing herself into Ben's arms. Sarah could hear her sobbing as she held onto him for dear life.

"Ben! Thank God you're all right! How's Jake?" She turned and came over to put her arm around Sarah's shoulders. "How are you doing?" Noticing the tears in her sister's eyes, Everly pulled her into her arms.

"He's strong, Sarah. But he needs you to stay strong so you can help him." She stepped back, holding her sister's shoulders in front of her. Just then, they could hear moaning coming from Jake's room. As Sarah ran into the room, she could see him trying to get out of the bed.

"What do you think you're doing, Jake Montgomery? Get yourself back onto that bed right now or so help me, you'll be sorry!" She was so angry at seeing him trying to get up that she left no doubt in anyone's mind that she meant business. He sat back down; looking at her with a feeble attempt at a grin, but the pain was too much. He grimaced as he grabbed his leg and fell back onto the bed.

By now, Everly was coming in with the boiling water and some cloths. She handed them to Sarah who told them both she'd take care of Jake. They left him in her care and went to sit in the other room.

Jake's eyes were squeezed shut and she knew he was in more pain than he was even letting on. She knew if he weren't, he would've been making some comment to her about her attitude or trying to embarrass her at his lack of clothing. She noticed he did at least make an attempt to cover himself as much as he could, while leaving his leg out to be tended to.

"This might hurt a little, Jake, but I have to clean your wound. I need to try and stop some of the bleeding." He nodded, his head lying on the pillow, keeping his eyes clenched shut.

She dipped the cloth into the water then wrung it out before laying it on his leg. He flinched as the hot water touched his wound. "I'm sorry, Jake." She carefully cleaned around the wound, dipping the cloth back into the water over and over until she looked down and noticed how red the pot of water had become. She almost cried out loud, wondering how much blood he'd lost.

Everly must have been hearing her thoughts, because she walked back into the room with another pot of boiled water. She bent down by her sister, giving her shoulder a squeeze as she left the new pot and removed the old one.

When she left, Sarah went back to holding the cloth onto the wound. She'd sat for what seemed like hours with her hand holding the cloth, feeling the blood soak through. Assuming Jake had passed out from the pain again, she was surprised when she looked up and caught him watching her.

"Don't think you'll be getting rid of me that easily. Although, I'm fairly certain there have been a few times you would've enjoyed putting a bullet in me since you got here." He tried to smile and make a joke, but she was too upset to be baited.

"I would never have wished this on you, Jake! Never!" She was almost in tears again, and he reached his hand out to set it on top of hers.

"I know, darlin', I was only trying to make you smile."

Just then, the door flew open and Everly was showing the doctor in to the room. He sat down to inspect the wound, and started giving orders for what he'd need. Sarah backed towards the door, unsure now what she should do. Jake kept his eyes on hers, giving her a wink as the doctor told her to go boil some more water and grab some towels.

Glad for something to do, she turned and fled from the room. The doctor was going to try removing the bullet and he needed her to get Ben to help hold him down.

When he had everything he needed, she sat with Everly in the other room. Hearing him scream in agony, she knew exactly when the doctor had started. She was glad it didn't last long though, as she assumed he'd passed out again from the pain. At least she hoped.

She sobbed in her sister's arms as they listened, and she was sure she was feeling the pain herself.

Finally, the doctor and Ben came out. Ben was whiter than the curtains on the window. "Well, I managed to get the bullet out, but I'm afraid he's lost a great deal of blood. It will be up to him now to heal, and we'll just have to hope he didn't lose too much blood or that he doesn't get an infection. His body might not be able to fight any infection, so you'll need to do your best to keep the wound clean."

The doctor was talking to her, as she was already walking back into the room to see Jake. She needed to see him for herself, and she was determined that she'd do whatever she had to do to get him better.

She never even heard the others leave, as she pulled the chair up next to his bed, took his hand in hers, and laid her head on top of them.

If it was true that love could heal everything, she was ready to give him all she had.

CHAPTER 11

The next few days, Sarah felt like she was living in a thick fog. She only left Jake's side long enough to boil water to wash him with, or to grab something to eat. Jake was in and out of consciousness as an infection set in to his leg.

Dr. Corbet had come back to see him, and said all they could do was try to keep the fever down, keep cleaning the wound the best they could, and hope for the best. Jake had lost a lot of blood during the ride home, and it was taking away a lot of the strength he might've had to fight against the infection.

Sarah sat next to the bed, and draped her body to lay her head down on the mattress. As she lay there listening to Jake's restless breathing, she felt a hand on her shoulder. She hadn't heard anyone come in, so she snapped her head up to see who was in the room. Seeing her mother standing there, she leapt up from her chair and flew into her mother's outstretched arms.

"Momma! You're here!" Sarah was sobbing. Never having realized just how badly she needed her mother at a time like this, seeing her standing there had brought so much emotion bubbling to the surface that she'd been trying so hard to fight these past days.

Her Momma just held her, stroking her hair like she did when she was a little girl. When she finally composed herself, she pulled back to look at her mother's face. "I didn't even know you were coming!" She'd never been so happy to see anyone in her life.

Her mother smiled at her. "I know. But, when Alistair got the wire from you asking for annulment papers and your money from the trust, I knew something had to be wrong. We were packing up and getting ready to come when we got another wire from Everly saying Jake had been shot. We were on the next train heading this way."

She looked towards where Jake was laying in the bed. "How is he?"

Sarah tried not to start crying again as she explained to her mother. The exhaustion she was feeling, along with the emotion of seeing her mother, was making it hard. She looked at her husband lying in the bed. "They managed to get the bullet out of his leg, but he lost an awful lot of blood before the doctor got to him. He was awake for a bit when they brought him home, but he's been in and out of consciousness the last two days. The infection is causing him to suffer quite badly, and when he does wake up, I don't think he's even aware of what's going on, or where he is." Her voice broke as she thought of the times he'd woken up, moaning in agony. Sarah had soothingly talked to him, placing cool cloths on his forehead trying to ease his discomfort.

"Everly says both her and Ben have tried to get you to rest and take turns tending to him, but that you refuse and won't let them help." Her mother was looking at her with raised eyebrows. "How do you suppose you'll be able to continue caring for him if you end up sick from exhaustion?"

"I'm his wife, Momma. I can't just leave him."

She turned to go to the other room so their talking wouldn't disturb him.

She saw Alistair sitting in the chair across the room, and she ran over to hug him. He stood when he saw her, putting his arms out to her. "Mr. McConnell, I'm so happy to see you!" Other than her own father, who she only saw from time to time growing up, Alistair McConnell had been the only man they'd known when they were children. Her father had never been a true father to them, so as their father's solicitor and friend, Alistair had stepped up and been the one man they could all count on.

"And I'm happy to see you, Sarah." He held her out in front of him. "How are you doing? You look like you haven't slept a wink in days." He scowled as he took in her disheveled appearance.

"I've slept a bit. I just stay in the chair next to Jake's bed in case he needs anything." She knew she looked a fright, but she hadn't wanted to crawl into the bed in case she rolled onto him and caused him any more pain. So, she'd just stayed in the chair next to the bed where she'd be close by to tend to him.

"Well, young lady. Your Momma and I are here now, so you can take yourself off and have a rest.

Get yourself cleaned up and if Jake needs anything, we'll come and get you." Alistair was giving her an order, and just because he was saying it in a calm voice, she knew he wasn't going to put up with any argument.

The only other place to sleep was in the barn, but Sarah suddenly felt ready to collapse with exhaustion, so she agreed to go and lay down for awhile. She peeked in on Jake and saw that he was still resting. She noticed he had more sweat on his brow, so she asked her mother to please put another cold cloth on his forehead.

Her mother put her hands on her shoulders and steered her towards the door. "He'll be fine, Sarah. I promise. Now go get some sleep!" Her Momma kissed her cheek, and then firmly pushed her out the door.

Sarah smiled for the first time in days. Her Momma had always been able to fix anything. She truly hoped this was one of those things.

IN HER DREAM, she was sitting on a blanket and laughing with Jake at a picnic. Everyone was there, and she was sure she'd burst with happiness. He pulled her up into his arms, swinging her around before setting her down and kissing her. She felt so loved; she never wanted it to end.

Suddenly, she could feel her shoulder being shaken. She wasn't ready to wake up; she wanted to stay where she was. "Sarah. Sarah! Jake needs you." Her mother's voice finally broke through, and she shot up, throwing her legs over the side of the bunk before she was even fully awake.

"What's the matter?" She was sliding her feet into her shoes and standing up to run to the house.

"He's just very unsettled. He must have sensed that you weren't there, and he's been calling for you. We didn't want to bother you, but we don't want him to cause any more problems with his wound. We did let you get some sleep before coming to get you." Her mother was walking fast alongside her as they made their way back to the house.

She felt her mother grab hold her of arm, stopping her. When she looked at her, she could tell she wanted to say something else. "What is it, Momma?" Her heart felt like it had stopped beating.

"Alistair brought the annulment papers. Are you sure this is what you want? From what I've seen since I got here, it appears as though you're very much in love with your husband. And, I haven't seen Jake awake enough to decide his feelings one way or another, but if the fact that he only seems settled when you're in the room is any indication, I'd have to say he's got some feelings for you as well." Her Momma didn't beat around the bush when she had something to say.

Sarah had forgotten all about the papers she'd asked Alistair to prepare. She looked out across the fields of green pasture, taking in the beauty of it all as she tried to gather her thoughts.

"I don't know anymore, Momma. At first, I figured we'd be able to make it work over time. But he just never seemed willing to let me in to his life. I know I cost him a lot when he was forced to marry me, and I need to repay him somehow. I thought I could give him his freedom back, as well as his prized stallion he had to give up for me, so he could move on with his life." She still hadn't moved or looked at her mother.

"Sometimes, just before he got hurt and when he was awake a few times since, I've thought maybe there might still be a chance." She looked towards her mother. "But how do I know it isn't just me wishing it to be true?"

Her mother put her arms around her shoulders and started to lead her back up toward the house. "Your heart will let you know, Sarah." She felt her mother squeeze her tight, and she looked up into her smiling face. "And I would hazard to guess it already has."

When they got in the house, she ran straight to Jake's room where she could hear him mumbling. As she entered the room, she could see the blankets spread all over as he thrashed around the bed. When he saw her, Mr. McConnell looked ready to flee and leave her to deal with it. If she didn't know Jake was in so much pain, she might have found the situation quite funny as Alistair desperately tried to calm the man in the bed.

"It's okay, Mr. McConnell, I can take over now." She smiled at the man who was obviously terribly uncomfortable at trying to soothe an injured man.

Hearing her voice, Jake stopped thrashing immediately. Without opening his eyes, he called for her with a raspy voice. "Sarah, is that you?" She went over and took his hand, sitting back in the chair she'd sat in for over two days now.

"It's all right, Jake, I'm here." She squeezed his hand, and she was sure she felt a faint squeeze back as he lost his battle with consciousness again.

Her Momma and Alistair stood in the doorway smiling at her. "We're staying at Ben and Everly's if you need anything. It looks like you have things under control here. I'll send Beth over later with something for you to eat."

Sarah smiled back at them, as she curled her legs up under herself to get more comfortable. When she heard the door close, she let herself sink back in and try to get back to her dream. She must have nodded off for awhile, and when she awoke, she saw that Jake was still resting comfortably. He seemed to not be as hot, and he hadn't been thrashing about at all since she got back. She hoped it meant he was getting through the worst of it.

Massaging her neck, she got up to make herself a cup of tea. She thought she'd get some more cool cloths to change the ones on Jake's forehead while she was up.

When she went into the kitchen, she saw some papers on the table. She went over and realized they were the annulment papers her mother had told her they brought. She sat down hard in the chair as she felt her hands shaking. What was she going to do now? Could she just give up on what she thought was starting to build between them?

She promised herself that she wouldn't decide anything until Jake was better. After it all, if he still seemed unable to care for her, she would do that for him. She knew she'd do anything to make him happy, even if it cost her heart.

CHAPTER 12

Sensing Jake was finally out of the woods, Sarah was able to breathe a little easier. He'd woken up a few times since her mother left earlier, and had been able to drink some water. He asked her what day it was, then cursed when he was told he'd been laying in bed for a few days now. He wasn't a good patient when he was awake, insisting he was fine and needed to get up. When she adamantly refused to let him up, he wasn't happy.

But, she figured it was a good sign to see him so ornery. It meant he was feeling better.

He was sleeping again now, still so weak from the blood loss. At least the fever had finally broken, so hopefully he was past the infection.

There was a knock at the door, which startled her. Most people she knew around here just walked in unannounced. She walked out to the other room, opening the door to see Sheriff Dixon standing there.

He was a nice looking man, with reddish gold hair that hung in his eyes when he took his hat off in greeting. "Howdy, ma'am. Sorry to disturb you when you obviously have your hands full with your husband's injury. I stopped over at Ben and Everly's first to make sure it'd be all right to call in here." Sarah opened the door wider and welcomed him inside.

"Can I get you a drink? I was just about to make myself some tea." She walked over to set some water on the stove to boil.

"No thanks. I won't keep you for too long. I just wanted to stop by and let Ben and Jake know that we think we caught the rustlers that shot your husband. They've been wanted around these parts for a long time now." He was watching her closely as he added, "We think they might be working for the Barlows."

She dropped her spoon onto the table, then sat down in the closest chair. The thought that she'd now also caused Jake to get shot was racing through her mind. Hank Barlow wanted to get even with Jake, and he'd sent those men to steal the cattle knowing Jake would come after them.

She felt like the floor had dropped out from under her.

Sheriff Dixon walked over and crouched in front of her. "We haven't been able to prove it for sure, but we have good reason to believe it. But, you can't blame yourself for any of this. Hank Barlow and your husband have a long history of hating each other, long before you even got here." He reached out to pat her hand, and she looked at him with a weak smile. How had he been able to tell what she'd been thinking?

He stood back up, then moved to the chair across the table. "And that's why I wanted to come today and make sure you changed your mind about going to the Barlows to buy back that stallion. I'm sure Jake wouldn't want you risking anything just for a horse."

The water on the stove had started to boil, but she hadn't even heard it. Sheriff Dixon got up, poured the water into her cup and brought it over to set in front of her.

"I know it's just a horse, but it was one Jake worked so hard to get. I need to try and get it back, to pay him back for everything he did to save me from the horrible fate that would have waited for me if I'd ended up married to Hank. And now, to know that I possibly caused him to get shot as well...." Her voice trailed off, as the other man interrupted.

"Sarah. I'm telling you the truth when I say you weren't responsible. You can't take this on your shoulders. Those two have been butting heads for as long as I've been here."

He continued, "And, I can't in good conscience let you go to the Barlow Ranch to get that horse. If you're still determined you're going to get it, I'll be with you. They gave me their price, and I'm almost sure it will use all of your father's trust he left you. It's far more than the horse is worth, but I can see you're probably going to pay it regardless." He was looking her in the eye, not letting her argue that she didn't need his help.

She nodded at him, and he sighed. Dragging his fingers through his tousled hair, she could tell he was annoyed that she was still going through with it even after his warning.

"Fine. I'll send word for them to meet outside my office in High Ridge tomorrow morning. I'll be there to make sure they don't try anything funny with you. Can you get away for a few hours tomorrow to come in?"

"I'll figure out a way. Thank you Sheriff Dixon. I appreciate your help in this matter."

"Call me Nate. And ma'am, it's no trouble at all. I just hate to see the Barlows getting away with that much money for a horse they never paid for. Doesn't seem right to me, but I guess that's none of my business." He smiled, then told her he'd see her in the morning.

She sat at the table while her tea went cold. She needed to figure out how to get into town in the morning without anyone stopping her. As she sat thinking of a plan, she heard a noise from the other room. Realizing that Jake was trying to get up again, she ran into the room to stop him.

"Jake! Why can't you just do as I tell you and stay in that bed?" She stormed over to where he was sitting on the edge of the bed. He looked up at her with a wicked grin, then reached out to pull her towards him. She was surprised at the strength he had as she almost fell on top of him.

"Well, I missed my nurse. I was getting pretty lonely in here. I might be better convinced to stay in bed if I had some company..." His voice was much stronger, and she almost wondered if he was caught by the fever again the way he was talking.

She pushed at his shoulders trying to stand up straight again. He just sat smiling up at her while keeping his hands around her waist. Caught in his stare, she could feel her knees starting to weaken. He must have sensed the moment she was at her weakest, because he pulled her down to him.

Reaching up to cup her face, he put his lips on hers. "I like it better when you're here." He was smiling as he kissed her. His lips started pushing harder, as he pulled her even closer. Before she knew it, she was laying beside him on the bed. Unsure how it had even happened, she worried that he might have hurt his leg again.

She struggled to sit up, "Jake, be careful or you're going to hurt yourself!"

He wasn't letting her go. "Sarah. What have you done to me?" That was all he said before his lips crushed hers again, this time leaving no doubt that he was fine. She tried to resist him, sure he was still too weak, and possibly even still suffering from the delirium of the fever, but she couldn't stop herself from responding.

He pulled back to look deep in her eyes. Without saying a word, he was asking her if he could continue. His fingers stroked her back, leaving her skin tingling beneath his touch. As she looked at him with all the love she felt in her heart, she reached up to gently caress his face. He groaned then brought his lips back down to hers.

At this moment, she didn't care what the future held for them. All she knew was that the man who held her in his arms was going to be all right, and he needed her right then as much as she needed him. Everything else could wait.

THE EARLY MORNING light was just making its way into the room, as Jake lay watching Sarah sleep. He fought the urge to reach out and caress her cheek, knowing how badly she needed to sleep. While he was in and out of consciousness over the past few days, he'd seen her sitting at his side. More than once, he'd seen her lying with her head down on the mattress, holding his hand while she hunched over from her chair.

He'd heard her crying, and fought hard to wake up, wanting to reassure her that he was going to be all right. So many times over the past days, he'd known she was there, and her presence beside him filled his heart with something he never thought he would feel.

She smiled in her sleep, and he pulled her closer to his chest. Closing his eyes, he fell back to sleep, content and happier than he'd ever been in his life. The woman in his arms had given him so much more than he deserved, and he intended to let her know how sorry he was for treating her so badly since the day she got there. She'd spent every day trying to make it up to him, and he was surprised she hadn't given up on him and left.

As he started to doze off, his last thoughts were how he planned to fall asleep with her in his arms every night for the rest of his life.

He woke up with a start; sure he'd only fallen asleep for a few minutes. The sun was shining brightly in the window, causing him to squint his eyes as he tried to get his bearings. He looked to the bed beside him, and saw that Sarah was already up. Smiling to himself, he lay back down with his arms behind his head. He knew she'd get angry with him if he tried getting up on his own, so he lay there waiting for her to come back in the room.

And, if he accidentally pulled her back in to join him for the rest of the day, there certainly wouldn't be any harm in that.

Not hearing any noise in the other room, he started to wonder if she'd gone out of the house. Deciding to risk her wrath, he sat up on the edge of the bed. He stood up and stretched. Lying in bed had sapped his strength, so he needed to get his muscles moving again.

He carefully pulled his pants on, wincing as the fabric rubbed his wound. He walked into the kitchen expecting to see Sarah standing at the stove or sitting in the chair. When he didn't see her, he walked over and opened the door. He walked out onto his front porch, breathing deeply of the fresh air he'd missed. He sat down on one of the chairs and waited to see where she'd gone.

After sitting there for awhile, he started to get worried. There was no sign of her anywhere. He walked over to the barn, giving his legs a much needed stretch. He searched inside and out, but she wasn't there. He headed back up to the house, starting to walk a little faster as he got closer. Where was she?

He got inside, and called her, but she didn't answer. She hadn't left his side for days, why would she leave now?

He started to feel sick inside. Maybe she hadn't

wanted to share his bed with him last night. What if he'd hurt her?

He sat down in the chair she used for mending all his clothes. He'd never once said thank you to her for any of it either. He put his head in his hands, wracking his brain to come up with a plan to find her. He just needed to rest for a minute. As he sat there, he noticed some papers sticking out of the basket with her mending. Reaching down, he pulled them out.

He felt like he just had the wind knocked out of him. So that was where she'd gone. He was looking at annulment papers that she obviously had drawn up, wanting to get out of their marriage. He couldn't say he blamed her, but he'd thought she would have at least talked to him about it.

He could feel his anger rising. How dare she think she could just walk away from him like it was nothing. And, if she thought about it, after last night, her grounds for stating the annulment was possible were gone. But, if that's what she wanted, then that's what she'd get. He'd let her out of this marriage.

Walking to the door to get his hat, he noticed a piece of paper set on the table. He walked over and picked it up. It was a note from Sarah saying she had to run into town for a few supplies, but she'd be back as soon as she could. She said Everly would be over this afternoon to make sure he didn't need anything.

He growled as he remembered the last time she'd taken off into town without him. She was up to something again, of that he had no doubt.

Crumpling the paper in his fist, he threw it to the ground. Turning to the door, he moved as fast as his leg would allow. Grabbing his hat, he stormed out the door. Just because he was willing to let her have her annulment, she didn't need to think she could get away from him that easily.

$\mathcal{A}$s they got closer to High Ridge, Sarah started to feel knots in her stomach. She knew Jake wouldn't be happy when he got up and found that note, but she hoped that when he saw her come back with his horse, he'd understand. Last night, she realized he did have feelings for her and that gave her hope for their future. He'd been so tender and loving; she had felt like she'd burst with happiness.

She wanted to get this over with so she could get back home into his arms. They finally would be able to build a future together.

Alistair had insisted on coming in with her when she rode over to ask for the papers to withdraw the money from her trust. He said he needed to be there to witness anyway, so told her to stop arguing because he was going with her no matter what she said.

She was glad to have him with her. He'd always done his best to take care of them, and she was so glad he and her mom had finally let their feelings for the other show.

"Are you sure you want to do this, Sarah? It isn't too late." He was looking at her intently, not happy about her decision to spend her entire trust fund on a horse.

"I don't need the money for anything else, Mr. McConnell. All I want is to get Jake's horse back; the one thing that still reminds me of how much he had to give up to save me from Hank Barlow." She wasn't going to back out now. "Then he and I can move past all of this and try to build some kind of future together."

He shook his head. "Well, let's get this over with then." Kicking his heels into his horse's side, he led the way into town. He headed straight for the sheriff's office, where they could see Nate Dixon standing outside waiting for them. As they pulled up, Nate reached out to help Sarah dismount.

"I see you didn't come to your senses." Nate

offered a smile as he helped her down, although she sensed that he was being very serious.

Just as Alistair was hopping down and tying the horses to the post, they could hear the sound of hooves on the dirt road. They all turned and saw Stewart and Hank Barlow riding up the street, leading the beautiful black stallion of Jake's.

Sarah noticed Alistair move closer to her, while Nate moved to stand between her and the men riding up. As she watched, she also noticed how the sheriff seemed to tense up at the sight of them. She sensed they had some kind of history together as she saw his fists clench at his sides while they waited for them to get closer.

The Barlow men were grinning as they pulled up, knowing how much the people there hated the fact they were about to get a very nice payout for this horse.

"I'm hurt that you didn't want to come out to my home directly, Sarah. We didn't need to drag everyone else into this exchange." Hank leered at Sarah as he dismounted.

"Hank, you know we'd never have let a women head out to your ranch on her own. Meeting here was my idea, so we can all make sure everything is done legally and without any trouble. Just hand

over the horse, and we'll get you your money."
Nate wasn't going to sit around and let them make
small talk, especially when anything they'd have to
say wouldn't be civil.

Hank and Stewart laughed, enjoying the looks
on the faces of everyone there.

Alistair walked over with the papers that signed
the money over to Hank, while Nate took Atlas's
reins and led him over to the other side where
Sarah was standing.

"You have your money, so you're free to leave."
Nate dismissed them, wanting to get Sarah back
out of town with the horse without any more
trouble.

As the men were about to hop back onto their
horses, they could hear the sound of hooves racing
up the street. Hank was the first to see who it was.
"Well, well. Looks like your husband didn't want to
miss the party." He was grinning, knowing how
angry Jake looked.

Sarah felt her heart drop. As soon as she saw
his face, she could tell how upset he was. He was
mad, and he was about to let her know.

"Does anyone here want to tell me just what the
hell is going on?" He was yelling the words before
he even got his horse stopped. "And, do you want

to tell me what you thought you were going to do with these?" As he stopped his horse and jumped down, he threw some papers towards Sarah.

She knew immediately he'd found the annulment papers. And, he had already jumped to the worst possible conclusion.

"Jake, just listen to me. I asked Mr. McConnell to draw those up for me long ago, when you were still making it clear to me that you didn't want to be married!" She was reaching for his arm, begging him to understand. He was too angry and she could see he wasn't going to listen.

He turned toward the Barlows. "And what business do you two have with my wife that I wasn't told about?" She could see the look of pure joy on Hank's face as he realized how angry Jake was, and knowing he was the cause of so much trouble for the man he hated.

"Oh, did your new bride not tell you all about our business arrangement? I'm surprised that a wife would be so disobedient to her husband already!" He was laughing, and it was making Jake see red.

Realizing he was pushing Jake a bit too far, he backed away while he continued. "Listen man, your wife was the one who contacted me. She just bought your horse back, and for a pretty penny, I might add." He held up the paper from Sarah's trust fund that showed the exact amount.

"She won't be paying you anything. I don't need the damn horse."

"Well, that's too bad. Shame you didn't get here just a bit sooner. The money has already exchanged hands, and the horse has been handed over." Stewart Barlow sauntered over while he let Jake know it was too late.

Sarah saw Jake clench his jaw together, and noticed the muscles in his cheek twitching as he turned back to face her. He looked at her for what seemed like an eternity before he finally spoke. "You just paid these snakes that much money; money that I assume was your entire trust fund left by your father, for a horse?" He was slowly walking toward her, and she backed up unsure what he was going to do next.

"I had to Jake. You lost that horse because of me." Putting the words into the simplest possible statement, she hoped he would understand.

"It's just a horse, Sarah. I would have got him back myself somehow anyway. But you never thought to ask me. Instead, you take it upon your-self to throw a ridiculous amount of money out to my biggest rivals in the entire state. What do you suppose they will now do with all that money?"

She felt the blood rush from her face. She hadn't even thought about that, but she immediately knew that the Barlow's had. She could hear their laughter as she stood staring at Jake who she noticed was looking very pale himself.

"But, I knew how much that horse meant to you, I never thought...." She was cut off as Jake turned back to the men.

"You both have what you came here for, so get on your horses and ride out of here."

"Oh, but we don't want to miss anything else! Looks like you have your hands full with this one. Guess I can thank my lucky stars you fell right into our hands and took her off mine." As soon as he said the words, Hank must have realized he'd said too much, because he shot a quick glance toward his father who was standing grinning like a cat who had swallowed a mouse.

Jake inched towards Hank. "What do you mean, fell into your hands?" He was backing the other man into the wall of the building, and Hank was quickly looking around for an escape. Stewart walked up to the men.

"Well Jake, the plan was for Hank to marry

the woman we knew you had a soft spot for, but you decided to show up and make things even more interesting." Stewart was keeping himself just behind Nate, hoping the sheriff would at least step in and help him if Jake got physical with him.

Now that Jake had turned his attention toward his father, Hank stepped back onto the street and felt safe enough to continue. "We heard from the wonderful woman who works in the mercantile here in High Ridge that she thought you had a liking for the sister that had spent some time out here before your cousin Ben got hitched. Oh, what was her name..."

"Hazel Hayes no doubt." Jake filled in for him through clenched teeth.

"Yes! That's her name. Anyway, we decided it might be fun to steal another woman from under your nose. Hank would get himself a wife, and it'd cause you even more suffering. Much as it did when Hank managed to take Anna from you." Stewart had taken over the story, enjoying the look on Jake's face as the words were sinking in.

Sarah was still standing rooted to the spot. She couldn't even make a sound as the reality of everything started to sink in. She'd been nothing but a naive pawn in some sick game the Barlows were playing with Jake.

"But, how...? How could you have known I'd even answer an ad from you?" She could barely speak above a whisper, and it took a few moments before anyone even heard her.

"Don't you remember, my dear? Think back to the day you bought the magazine that had Hank's ad....was there anyone else around you spoke to? Anyone else who might have pointed you in the direction of the ad?" Stewart Barlow was enjoying every minute of the attention he was getting from the shocked people around him.

Sarah swallowed hard as she realized all eyes were on her. She could feel her lip trembling as she remembered the man who'd been in the mercantile in Chicago all those weeks ago. He'd seemed like such a nice older man, and he'd asked her if she was thinking of answering an ad as she flipped through the pages, trying to decide if she should answer an ad.

It was the day after she'd heard her Momma talking to Mr. McConnell and she thought she'd try to find someone like Ben.

He'd smiled so kindly and flipped through the pages with her for awhile, finally pointing one out that he said sounded perfect. Of course, it was Hank's ad.

She moved her eyes to Jake, unable to believe how she'd been duped into helping to destroy his life. She didn't even know what to say, sure there was nothing that could be said anyway. Everything had been a set up, with her playing into their hands with ease.

She'd cost Jake everything and the reality of it all was too much for her. She spun on her heels and hopped onto the horse that she'd just bought back for Jake. She knew he was the fastest, and all she wanted was to get as far away as she could.

All she could hear was Jake hollering, "Dammit Sarah -- stop!" as she raced down the street, hanging on for dear life. She didn't care about anything except getting away. As the horse flew towards the edge of town, she knew she'd made a mistake, she wasn't an experienced enough rider for the stallion, but she didn't care.

Hot tears were flowing down her cheeks as she felt herself being flung off the horse's back. As blackness took over, she thought at least now Jake would be free of the nightmare she'd caused him.

CHAPTER 14

*A*s her eyes started to flutter open, she could feel herself being lifted in strong arms. She was being carried, so gently, and she just wanted to stay asleep. Finally remembering what had happened, she looked up into the angry face of her husband. He had stubble around his chin from not shaving for the past few days, but he still looked so handsome to her.

Somehow sensing she was now awake, he looked down at her, and she noticed his eyes soften. "Are you all right, sweetheart?" He'd stopped walking, still just holding her in his arms.

All she could do was nod, unable to make words for fear of breaking down. He continued walking, while Nate opened the door to his office and the men all fussed to lay her down on the cot. She noticed Jake nod to the other men to leave, but she saw Mr. McConnell hold back, unsure if he should leave her in there alone with him.

She smiled to him to let him know she was okay. As he walked outside, she could hear Nate Dixon telling the Barlow's to get out of town before he found something to arrest them for.

She sat up, rubbing at her left arm which was hurting a bit from her fall. She couldn't look at Jake, but she knew he was standing there waiting for her to talk.

"Jake, I'm so sorry. I've just made such a mess of things. I never meant to cause so much disruption in your life, or to cost you so greatly..." She was desperately trying to find the words to say how sorry she was. He was still not saying anything, so she slowly raised her eyes to find his.

He was standing in front of her, with his head down and the pad of his hands pressing into his eyes. It was like he couldn't make himself look at her.

"I never knew that ad was set up meaning to hurt you. I would never have answered..." She was talking so fast now, just trying to get him to say something — anything.

As a tear rolled down her cheek, she saw him finally look at her. His eyes held so much emotion in them, she was unsure what to do.

He stepped closer to her, his eyes following the path of her tear. Reaching up to wipe it away with his thumb, he rested his forehead on hers.

"Sarah. When I saw you falling from that horse, I didn't care about any of it. Not the annulment, not the going behind my back to buy Atlas back, not even being forced to marry you. All I cared about was you being all right." His voice shook.

Pulling his head back to look in her eyes, he reached down and pulled her hands up to his chest. "All you have cost me darlin', is my heart."

Sarah felt a sob make its way out of her throat as she heard what he was saying.

"You may feel like you cost me everything by marrying you, but I'd do it all again in a heartbeat to be with you. I know I've been stubborn, and pigheaded, and likely not very nice to be around since we got married. I tried to pretend like I was put out, or like I'd done something noble at great cost to myself, when in truth, I was just too scared to admit that I wouldn't have let you marry another man no matter what the cost."

He was pleading with her to understand what he was saying, struggling to find the right words.

"Sarah, I've loved you long before you came back into my life at the hands of Hank. I was just too stubborn to admit it. Marrying you was no hardship to me. If I truly hadn't wanted to marry you, I would've got you away from Hank Barlow some other way. I'm sure you know by now that I'm not the kind of man who's ever forced to do anything he doesn't want to do."

His eyes looked deep into hers. He was holding her so close, she could feel his heart beating.

"Nothing else matters to me. If you'll have me, even after I've spent the past weeks making your life miserable, I'd love to spend the rest of my life trying to make it up to you."

"But Jake, you need to let me explain! The annulment, buying Atlas back..." She wished she hadn't said anything to break the moment, but she had to put everything out there so they could make things right.

"I told you, nothing else matters. Do you want to stay married to me?" He asked her so quietly, she was almost sure he was scared to hear her answer.

"That's all I've ever wanted, Jake!" She pulled

her hands from his, then put them on top to now place them on her own chest. "My heart has always been yours."

He moaned low in his throat, then pressed his lips down to hers. She felt a need in his kiss, which she returned. They had been through so much, and faced so many things trying to get between them, but she was now in his arms, and she could tell by the way he was holding her, he was never going to let her go.

Sarah pulled her head back, trying to regain some of her composure. Jake was breathing hard as he smiled down at her. He lifted his hand to caress her cheek.

"Now, if it's all right with you, Mrs. Montgomery, I would like to take you home and continue where we left off last night...." He chuckled at her as she felt the heat rise in her cheeks as she thought of the night she'd spent in his arms.

Deciding she better get used to living with a man who enjoyed trying to rile her up, she decided to give it back to him. Lifting her chin, she stepped away from him, grabbing his hand to pull him behind her.

"Mr. Montgomery, I think we better hurry

because I'm not sure if I want to wait even that long." She smiled the sweetest smile back at him as she enjoyed the look on his face.

THE WEDDING WAS BEAUTIFUL, everything set up in Ben and Everly's yard. Her Momma had been the most beautiful bride in the world, and Alistair had spent the day hovering over his new wife.

Sarah was dancing with her husband, tired after the long day of festivities.

Placing her head on his chest, he reached up and brushed the back of her hair with his hand. "Tired, darlin'?" He pushed her back enough that he could look in her eyes.

"Just happy," She smiled up at him. He was looking at her with a mischievous look, which usually meant she needed to be ready for something to happen.

"Jake Montgomery, what are you up to? It's been a long day, and I don't know if I have the energy to fight with you." She was trying to be stern, but she could tell he was excited about something.

As they stood in the middle of the dance floor,

the music suddenly stopped and it seemed like everyone was watching them. Jake stepped back, taking one of her hands in his. He was staring at her so intently, she couldn't move from her spot. Her eyes were searching his, waiting to see what he was up to.

Reaching in to his pocket, he pulled out a ring and started to place it on her finger. She gasped as she looked at it. "Sarah, I reckon it's about time we made it official. Will you marry me?" He was grinning at her like a little boy.

She looked around at the smiling faces all around her, and she felt like her world started spinning faster. "Well, what do you mean Jake? We're already married."

He spoke just loud enough for her to hear, bending his head down to meet hers. "No, I want you to have a real wedding. Not one that you ever feel wasn't what I wanted. I want you to have your first kiss, and I want you to hear the words we share to bind us together for life, said in love. I want you to have your happy ever after."

With that, he turned her around, and she saw Nate standing there waiting. He winked at her, "Jake thought I'd done such a good job the first time around, he asked me if I'd mind doing it a second time."

In a blur, they said their vows, until it came time for Jake to kiss his bride. He turned and pulled her close to him, bending his head down to meet hers. As they kissed, she could hear everyone around them cheering and clapping.

When he pulled his head back to smile down at her, with all the love she was feeling, she whispered, "You are, and always have been, my happy ever after."

*THANK you for reading my story about Sarah and Jake! I hope you enjoyed it. (If you could take a moment to leave a review - it would be greatly appreciated!)

IF YOU'D LIKE the next book in the series, BETH, you can find it under the Historical West-ern>>Wilder West Series page on my website at kaypdawson.com

. . .

Or, you can just open your smartphone's photo app and hold it up to the QR code below, which will bring the link up for you to click through directly to my website :)

There is also a short story - MAGGIE'S GIFT - which takes place between this story and the next. It's only available in Digital form, however you can read it on any device you have. (You don't have to read it to understand the next one, but it does give a happy ever after to someone you've met already ;) It's available to purchase or you can get it free on the newsletter subscribers-only page :)

. . .

IF YOU HAVEN'T ALREADY JOINED the mailing list - you can get a *free book just for signing up*! It features the diary writings of Caroline, the mother of the Wilder women, from the time she lost her parents until the time of Everly - Book 1 in the series.

KAYPDAWSON.COM/NEWSLETTER

Kay P. Dawson is a mom of two girls, who always dreamed of being a writer. After a breast cancer diagnosis in 2011, she decided it was time to follow her dream.

Years of reading historical romance, combined with her love for all history related to the old west and pioneer times, she knew that writing in the western historical genre was her calling.

Over time, she decided to add contemporary titles and even some time travel books to her catalogue - always incorporating small towns and family into her stories while the characters find their happy ever after.

She writes sweet romance, believing a good love story doesn't need to give all of the juicy details - a true love story shows so much more. So, whether the book is taking place back in the wild frontier or in present day, you will be taken to a special place where family, friends and communities always come together - and true love always finds a way.

You can connect with Kay through her website at **KayPDawson.com**

She also has an active fan group where she hangs out with her readers...https://www.facebook.com/groups/kaypdawsonfans/**

Newsletter SignUp:

http://www.kaypdawson.com/newsletter

Be sure to follow me on Bookbub to get notifications of any new releases or special discounts on my books!

https://www.bookbub.com/authors/kay-p-dawson

kaypdawson.com
kaypdawsonwrites@gmail.com

facebook.com/kaypdawsonauthor
twitter.com/KPDawsonAuthor

Printed in Great Britain
by Amazon

41019279R00094